What the critics are saying...

"I couldn't put it down until I finished it." - *Angel Brewer, Just Erotic Romance Reviews*

"A dark, mysterious tale with a couple of surprising turnabouts...the story fascinated and inspired me. It's just fantastic." - *Mon Boudoir*

"In addition to the steamy side of the story I really enjoyed how Ms Black speculated on the future of our planet, origins of ancient cultures like the Greeks and Egyptians as well as weaving in some references to possible origins of some enduring legends like the Amazons, vampires and gryphons. However, this was done with a light touch that left it to the readers' imagination to pick up and run with these ideas or concentrate on the many other aspects of the story. This is an excellent blend of suspense, sci fi and paranormal elements. Breeding Ground is Romantica™ at its best, a keeper to enjoy again and again. I highly recommend it." - *Patrice Storie, Just Erotic Romance Reviews*

D0710802

BREEDING GROUND
An Ellora's Cave Publication, September 2004

Ellora's Cave Publishing, Inc.
1337 Commerce Drive, #13
Stow, OH 44224

ISBN 1-4199-5128-9

ISBN MS Reader (LIT) ISBN # 1-84360-837-5
Other available formats (no ISBNs are assigned):
Adobe (PDF), Rocketbook (RB), Mobipocket (PRC) & HTML

Edited by *Heather Osborn.*
Cover art by *Darrell King.*

Warning:

The following material contains graphic sexual content meant for mature readers. *Breeding Ground* has been rated E–rotic by a minimum of three independent reviewers.

Ellora's Cave Publishing offers three levels of Romantica™ reading entertainment: S (S-ensuous), E (E-rotic), and X (X-treme).

S-*ensuous* love scenes are explicit and leave nothing to the imagination.

E-*rotic* love scenes are explicit, leave nothing to the imagination, and are high in volume per the overall word count. In addition, some E-rated titles might contain fantasy material that some readers find objectionable, such as bondage, submission, same sex encounters, forced seductions, etc. E-rated titles are the most graphic titles we carry; it is common, for instance, for an author to use words such as "fucking", "cock", "pussy", etc., within their work of literature.

X-*treme* titles differ from E-rated titles only in plot premise and storyline execution. Unlike E-rated titles, stories designated with the letter X tend to contain controversial subject matter not for the faint of heart.

BREEDING GROUND

JAID BLACK

PART I:
THE HAUNTING

PROLOGUE

She shivered from where she lay curled up in a ball on the red earthen floor, her arms wrapped around her up drawn knees, her eyes unblinking. She was cold, hungry, and broken—at last broken.

Just as *he* had planned. Just as *he* had always wanted.

He kept her in a cage, naked and half-starving, like a neglected animal in a zoo. Every day her will to resist him grew weaker and weaker. Every day the hunger gnawed at her belly until the pangs felt like sharp talons clawing at her gut.

She was weak. So fucking weak. She needed nourishment—food and water. Oh God, how she fantasized about water trickling down her dry, parched throat...

She would never be given water unless she did what he wanted.

No, she thought in horror. *How can I let that...that...thing touch me? How can I —*

"I would have your answer," he purred.

She closed her eyes against the sound of his voice. She was so frail that not even her hearing worked as acutely as it once did, for she hadn't realized until he'd spoken that he'd approached the cage. She could feel his devil's-eyes on her, though, just like always. Coiled up in a ball with her back to him, she still knew the precise moment when his eerie golden gaze flicked to her buttocks...and then onward to the folds of flesh visible between her legs.

That flesh was what he wanted. That and a whole lot more. He wanted things from her that were so sick and frightening they didn't bear dwelling on.

"Answer me," he hissed, "or I leave you here for another night."

By the morning she would be dead. And escape would be a moot point. Her body was so damn weak...

"Yes," she whispered. She closed her eyes tighter, feeling ill. "I've just consented to being the devil's whore."

His depraved laughter echoed throughout the underground cavern, reverberated against the impenetrable bars of the cage. "Much lower than a whore," he murmured. "At least a whore is permitted to live through it."

She wanted to vomit, could feel bile churning in her belly.

"Look at me!" he shouted, his voice angry. "You will look at me!"

Oh no—oh please no.

She drew her knees up impossibly closer against her breasts. She didn't want to look at him. Anything but that. Sweet God above, anything but—

"Look at me!" he bellowed.

And then he was in the cage, his hideous claws jerking her up from the ground, forcing her to her feet. She wanted to fight him, but she could barely speak or stand, let alone rage against him.

"Look at me!" he demanded, shaking her. "Open your eyes!"

No! No! No! Oh God, please don't make me look at him!

She'd never been more frightened. Her heart was thumping like a rock against her chest, her breathing sporadic and growing more labored by the second. She was afraid to know what he looked like for she'd seen his kind before. Hideous. Freakish.

Monsters.

"I said look at me!"

Her nostrils flared in challenge as her eyes flew open. Her gaze clashed with serpentine gold-slitted eyes.

Oh God...

"Nooooo!" she screamed. "Nooooo!"

Alex gasped as she bolted upright in bed, her breathing heavy, the sheets soaked with her perspiration. Her eyes darted frantically about as they adjusted to her surroundings—and to the fact that she had been asleep.

"Just a dream," she breathed out, her eyes wide. "Just a nightmare."

Exhausted, she fell back onto the bed, expelling a breath of air as she did so. Three times in six months she'd entertained bizarre nightmares, though this one had been far more detailed than the others before it.

She had almost gotten to see what *it* looked like.

"What does it matter?" she murmured to the four walls. She sighed, closing her eyes. "It was only a dream."

Part II:
Descent Into Hell

CHAPTER ONE

"Houston, the *Methuselah* has successfully left the Robert Frazier galaxy and is beginning its long-awaited return to the Milky Way."

Dr. Alexandria Frazier grinned into the microphone. She wondered what Robert would have thought about her naming a galaxy after him. The way she figured it, she had that right. She'd discovered the damn thing after all.

Robert...she sighed. In Earth time he'd been dead for over fifteen hundred years. But only two years had passed aboard the *Methuselah*, so she still considered herself recently widowed. Her husband lived on in her memories as though he'd made love to her only yesterday...or only two years ago as it were.

Dr. Robert Frazier's death during a routine flight to Europa XII, the space station that had been erected on Jupiter's largest moon, had been as devastating to Alex as it had been unexpected. NASA had short trips like that down to an art form. Finding out that he'd died while taking pressurization readings in the cargo area aboard the spaceship he'd been traveling on had seemed like a cruel joke.

During a meteor shower—okay. While exploring alien terrain for signs of life—okay. But while taking pressurization readings?

Alex took comfort in the knowledge that Robert had died instantaneously. He'd died not knowing he was going to die. He never experienced fear, remorse, or any of the other countless emotions someone who knew they were about to meet their maker no doubt experienced. In that way, Robert had been lucky. It was all the comfort Alex had to hold onto, so she'd clung to it fiercely from the first day of her widowhood onward.

It had been her husband's untimely death that had spurred Alex into signing up for the mission she was currently completing. NASA had been hard-pressed to find qualified volunteers for the first human journey into deep space, and for good reason. Doing so, after all, meant that the workers aboard ship would never again lay eyes on their homes and on the people from Earth they'd once cherished. Those places and loved ones would have been dead for over fifteen hundred years, remembered only by the explorers of the *Methuselah* and automated personal libraries.

As a result of that cold reality, mostly those with nothing and no one to lose had ended up going. The prospect of the journey was an exciting one to every scientist at NASA, but in the end most had decided against requesting passage. Alex's crew, of which she was the captain, consisted of seven human scientists and four almost freethinking droids.

"The date on Earth that we expect to land in Houston, or whatever Houston now is," Alex intoned into the microphone, her thoughts straying back to the work at hand, "is October 19, 3679 A.D., exactly one thousand five hundred years from the day we left. Today's date in Earth years is August 3, 2701 A.D." She sighed. "Though you probably won't receive this message via satellite for another fifty years."

Due to advances in technology prior to the Methuselah leaving Earth, it had only taken the crew twenty Earth years to reach deep space. The spaceship had ventured as deeply into the outer bounds as planned, so far out, in fact, that it would take a full thousand Earth years to return. Time and space were a confusing business.

Alex nestled into the high-backed chair, her thoughts turning to what her crew had managed to accomplish. They'd landed on fourteen different planets in three different solar systems and two different galaxies. The work they had done was important to all humans for they'd discovered habitable planets that Earthlings could reasonably colonize should the planet become overpopulated or contaminated — assuming it already hadn't.

She toyed with the microphone in her grasp as she absently stared out into the black abyss on the other side of the viewing window before her. Her voice had a reflective, faraway quality to it. "As much as I am loath to admit to a failure, Houston, I owe Robert a hundred bucks. He was right. Mankind *is* the most advanced life-form out here. Or, at least, is still the most advanced life-form known to us."

She ran a hand through the long blonde curls she usually kept rolled back into a confining bun at the nape of her neck. "We've discovered other life, of course, but none so advanced as the *Homo Sapiens Sapien.* The closest thing we have found to self-aware beings is a race of thinking creatures in Robert Frazier Galaxy. We named the planet Paleo and its race Paleoliths for they brought to mind the sort of primitive thinkers one would have expected to find in the beginning stages of human evolution. I'm sure if NASA were to make a return voyage a few hundred thousand years from now we would find beings on par with us." She smiled. "Or will they be on par with us? Perhaps humans have continued to evolve as well."

Alex's smile dissolved as she considered the answer to that question. "What kind of a world will the crew of the *Methuselah* find waiting for us upon our return?" she murmured into the microphone. "It is unlikely, from an evolutionary standpoint, that much has changed in the human genetic make-up in fifteen hundred years, though I suppose the possibility always exists. Medieval humans were, after all, significantly shorter in stature than humans of the Post-Information Age.

"But that doesn't worry me. So I might be considered a bit short when I get back to my beloved Earth..." She smiled. "I can live with that. What keeps me up at night is wondering what my home will look like."

She shook her head slightly, her light green eyes narrowed in thought. "I can't begin to imagine what sorts of changes will have occurred in the infrastructure of everything from the nuclear family to society as a whole to which country now owns what. Is the United States still a superpower? Does it wield the same worldwide influence it once did?"

Her forehead wrinkled. "These are the thoughts that plague me. The possible answers terrify me as much as they excite me..."

She took a deep breath and slowly released it. "In approximately two months the crew of the *Methuselah* is expecting to be able to pick up signals sent to us from Earth in the year 3010 A.D. That was the agreed upon date for transmission prior to embarking on this journey. We expect the images we receive to give us a hint of what sort of a world we are coming back to, though we are well aware of the fact that another six hundred years will have passed by on Earth by the time we disembark from this spacecraft."

Her gaze fell to the photograph of Robert she kept at her station. "My husband will have been dead for one thousand five hundred years, four months, six days, and twelve hours. It is almost unfathomable," she murmured, "but there it is."

Resting her head between her palms, Alex switched off the microphone and stared out into the nothingness beyond the window panel before her. In two months, she and her crew would have their answers. They would know what had become of the Earth they'd once called home. And Alex would know whether or not she owed Robert another hundred bucks.

She could only hope that she did.

CHAPTER TWO

"Come on, Peacock. You can block me better than that!"

Her breasts heaving up and down from labored breathing, Alex swiped at the perspiration trickling down her forehead with the back of her arm. Peacock was the only other third degree blackbelt on board, so they'd been sparring partners since the voyage had first begun. It was a NASA requirement to be in excellent physical condition, so every human on board sported well-honed musculature, but she and the P-man were the only two versed in karate. "Hell, my grandma could have blocked me better than that."

Lieutenant Treyson "Peacock" Williams half-grinned and half-frowned at Alex as he hunched over with a palm on either leg, trying to bring down his heart rate. "Maybe," he said between pants. "But I look a helluva lot better doing it."

Alex chuckled as she accepted a wet towel from Marax, the droid that had been accompanying her on missions since she'd flown her first one at age twenty-six. That was ten years ago now. The seven-foot tall cyborg looked more man than machine, the only noticeable differences being his programmed emotions, silver eyes, and bluish skin.

"Don't get soft on me," Alex teased, winking. She patted the cool wet towel against the back of her neck. "Or I'll have to start sparring with Marax again." She grimaced. "I'd rather not. Sometimes the big guy doesn't know when enough is enough."

Lt. Williams grinned fully, his handsome ebony face crinkling into a smile. "I'm sure I'll be back in form tomorrow, Alex. Even a man as fine as me has the occasional off day."

Alex rolled her eyes good-naturedly. "Why is it that we call you Peacock again?" She made a show of squinting her eyes and tapping a finger against her cheek. "Gee, if only I could remember…"

Peacock laughed as he patted her on the back. "Time for the mess hall, boss lady. It's chow time."

"Chow time," she grumbled as she followed the lieutenant from the ship's rec room. She frowned as the silver sensory door slid open, closing with a hissing sound behind them. "I wonder what tonight's delight will be? Soup, soup, or if we're lucky…hey, maybe soup!"

He snorted at that. "God's truth I can't wait to get home and have some real food. I've been dying for some of my mama's cooking for…" His voice trailed off. He took a deep breath and glanced away. "Well, I can't wait to get back home," he muttered.

Alex briefly put a hand on his shoulder to let him know she cared, but said nothing more on the subject. There was no point in it. All the crewmembers were going through the same thing. All of them were coming to terms with the cold, hard fact that life as they'd once known it would not exist when they disembarked. They didn't yet know what kind of a world they'd be stepping out onto. They could only hope it was a better one.

"Let's go eat," Alex said in the most upbeat tone of voice she could muster as they walked down the ship's south corridor together. "I'm in the mood for some soup. How about you?"

Peacock laughed, the sound as forced as Alex's cheerful voice. "Sounds like a plan, commander."

* * * * *

"And then she actually tried to fuck me if you can believe it. Jesus H. Christ, I thought I was gonna throw up for sure."

Alex genially shook her head as she listened to Dr. John Nielson recount the nearly disastrous run-in he'd had with one of the Neanderthal-like females they'd encountered back on planet Paleo. The creature had taken to John at first sight and had done her damnedest to try and keep him. She'd gone so far as to knock him out from behind then drag him back to her lair. It had taken four days for John to free himself of her, during which time he'd been thought dead by his teammates.

Two months ago it had been no laughing matter. She was glad the warrior-scientist had recovered enough from the ordeal to talk and even joke about it.

"How do you know she was trying to fuck you?" Lt. Williams asked, his expression serious. "Maybe she was—I don't know—having a seizure or something. Maybe that's what all the convulsing was about."

"Ah Peacock, come on, man!" John frowned. "As much as I would like to remember it that way, trust me when I say she was trying to impregnate herself. Her pupils were dilated and her vaginas were secreting some gross viscous shit."

"Goddamn," Peacock muttered. "That's fucking gross."

"Yeah, tell me about it." John grinned as he dunked a cracker into his beef stock soup. "I came that close to fathering a little hybrid, my friend."

"Yeeck! That is some twisted shit there. I think that—" Peacock's body stilled. His jaw slightly unhinged. "Wait a minute, bro. You said her vaginas, as in plural. You mean to tell me that thing had more than one pussy?"

John nodded. "Two of the ugliest, smelliest, hairiest pussies I've ever had the misfortune to lay eyes on."

Despite the rather repugnant turn the meal conversation had taken, Alex chuckled at Lt. Williams's horrified expression, a dimple denting her cheek. He looked ready to faint. Peacock might be six-feet four-inches of solid, deadly muscle, but, ever the Romeo, he was something of a soft touch where females were concerned. Apparently the lovemaking connoisseur had finally found a delicacy he didn't wish to partake of.

"Goddamn." The lieutenant shook his head, his lips puckered as though he'd just sucked on a lemon. "All I can say is god*damn*."

Alex grinned as she lowered the soupspoon from her lips. "Oh come on, Peacock," she teased. "I thought your motto has always been the more the merrier."

The crew broke into laughter. Peacock opened his mouth to make a rebuttal, but was interrupted by the sound of a loud, pulsing, warning tone blaring over the ship's intercom.

Alex dropped her spoon and flew to her feet. She was about to dash toward the main workstation of the *Methuselah* to find out what trouble was underfoot when a female droid assigned to the workstation entered the mess hall. The droid was outfitted the same as the human crew, her uniform a skintight black latex bodysuit. "Report, Phariz," Alex ordered. "What is the malfunction?"

The silver eyes of the blue droid found Alex's. "The satellite scanners aboard ship have retrieved an

unexpected signal from Earth, Commander Frazier,"
she stoically reported. "You are needed in Work Pod
3 immediately."

Alex's eyes rounded. She followed Phariz from
the mess hall, her pace brisk. She ignored the
murmurings of the crew following on her heels and
concentrated on getting from point A to point B. Not
that Alex could blame her crew for their collective
reaction. She was harboring the same bad feeling in
the pit of her stomach. Their ship, after all, wasn't
supposed to receive a transmission from Earth for
another six weeks.

"Is it possible it took less time to receive the
transmission than we expected?" This to Phariz. "Or
did Houston signal us hundreds of years before they
were supposed to?"

"Probability says the latter."

"Why?"

"Because the former explanation isn't linear.
According to the law of — "

"Never mind." Alex wasn't interested in a dry
explanation of physics from the droid. The
explanation didn't matter. If Phariz thought that
Houston had transmitted a signal to them hundreds
of years before they were scheduled to then they
probably had. The droid had yet to be wrong.

She frowned thoughtfully as the sensory door to
Work Pod 3 slid open. "According to probability,"
Alex said to Phariz as she dashed toward the

planning table, "what is the single most likely reason Houston would have to contact us early?"

The droid answered her question as if it was of no greater import than the weather. "To warn the *Methuselah* of a catastrophe."

"Damn," Alex heard John mutter. "I was afraid she was going to say that."

"Everybody sit down and shut up!" Alex shouted when the crew began speculating about the significance of the early signal amongst themselves. "Phariz, pull up the images Houston transmitted." She took her seat at the head of the round planning table and waited for the holographic display in the center of it to commence. "Let's find out what in the hell is going on," she muttered.

The work pod grew quiet enough to hear a pin drop. Alex's heart felt as though it might beat out of her chest. She realized that no good news would be forthcoming from the transmission. Without knowing to expect an incoming signal on a particular frequency, the odds of the *Methuselah* picking it up were one in a trillion. Houston had to have known that fact. That they'd opted to chance it and send one anyway didn't bode well.

By the time the holographic image of a bald man who looked to be in his early fifties appeared, perspiration was dotting Alex's forehead. The crew could only see the man from the waist-up, as he appeared to be seated in some sort of foreign looking winged-back chair.

"Greetings to you from the year 2792, Methuselah. This transmission is being sent two hundred and eighteen years prior to the pre-established rendezvous time. I am speaking to you from Zutair, the largest city-state in New France. Zutair is located in the area that was once called Houston, before the former United States fell to the French in the year of our lords 2686."

"No fucking way," Peacock mumbled, his eyes unblinking.

"I could see Germany," John added, wincing. "The Germans have always been some fierce mother-fuckers. I can even see Japan. But goddamn *France*?" His jaw clenched. "No way."

Alex threw both men a commiserating frown, then turned her attention back to the holographic image of the bald messenger.

"But Zutair is not transmitting to you today to tell you of the fall of the country you once called home, for New France welcomes you with the same open arms as the United States would have. Instead, Zutair has contacted you to warn you of—"

The transmission scrambled, inducing Alex to swear under her breath. "Get the signal back up, Phariz. Now!" When the transmission continued in the same fuzzy manner for another twenty seconds despite the droid's best efforts, she flew up to her feet. "Elinor!" she shouted out to the scientist aboard ship who was the best versed in holographicary in particular and transmission waves in general. "Can you unscramble the signal?"

"I'll try," Dr. Elinor Fitzsimmons-Ivanov threw over her shoulder as she dashed toward the mega-computer console two feet away. "I don't know what's jamming it. Shit! Vlad! Peacock! I need some help getting behind this thing. Can you move it?"

Twenty seconds later the mega-computer had been moved enough for the slight female scientist to get behind it and Elinor was busy fumbling with its wiring. "It's coming back up!" Alex announced, her heart rate over the top. "Okay it's back online! Good work, doctor."

Only the images they were now seeing were nonsensical. Apparently whatever part of the bald Zutairan man's speech they'd missed had been important.

"What the...?" John's forehead wrinkled. "A Paris fashion show in 2190. The invention of the 'nanny droid' in 2287—huh, she can breastfeed. Freethinking cyborgs in 2350. The resurgence of polytheistic religion in 2467..."

"We're being given a history lesson," Alex murmured. "Everybody pay close attention."

A worldwide stock market crash in 2675. Immediate pandemonium. The fall of the United States a decade later...

The images became almost too horrific to watch from that point onward. Alex's hand unconsciously flew up to cover her mouth as she learned what had become of the country she had once called home.

The stock market crash had affected the United States and Japan more drastically than any other countries. Both nations had risen to become the undisputed mega-powers of the world by the year 2499, a status way and beyond that of superpower. But because of their dramatic rise, the two nations apparently had the furthest to fall and therefore the most to lose.

And lose they both did.

Not wanting one to subvert the other during a time of vulnerability, the mega-powers had faced off, eventually turning their grotesque biological weaponry against the other. The effect was devastating.

Famine. Poverty. Disease. Complete and utter chaos.

Mutated offspring.

Alex shivered when images of deformed survivors filled the center console. Half-freak and half-human, the race of people that emerged from the ashes of biological warfare was hideous in appearance and more shocking than words could say. Their eyes looked crazed, their animalistic behavior maniacal.

"Jesus Christ," she heard John mutter. "Holy God."

France recuperated from the worldwide fallout the quickest and soon emerged as Earth's only mega-power. Within a decade the French army managed to drive the deformed race of humans underground and reestablish a semblance of normalcy for the entire globe. A globe which had, incidentally, been renamed New France in honor of its unlikely savior.

Alex stared surrealistically at the holographic image playing out before her. Wide-eyed, her stomach knotting, she was as shocked and dazed as her crew.

The images flash-forwarded to the year 2789— and to a new and far more horrific battle that was being fought, freak versus human.

The deformed humans had stayed underground for close to a century. For so long, in fact, that the people of Earth—or New France as it was—had believed they'd all died off from their hideous afflictions.

They had been wrong.

The freaks emerged from their lairs stronger and deadlier than before. Within six months they wrested control of the planet and it was now the humans who were forced into hiding. The holographic images glossed over most of the particulars, showing only the bare bones of the turmoil that had long since erupted.

"And so on this night, the eve of Armageddon, we send this final report to you not knowing what the outcome of the battle ahead will be."

Alex swallowed over the lump in her throat as the Zutairan man continued his speech.

"In roughly six hours time, the mobilized troops of New France will attack the demons' stronghold in the city-state of Tongor. If we can penetrate their stronghold, then we still have a chance at winning. If we cannot, then I leave you to speculate as to what has befallen humankind."

Alex threw a hand toward Phariz when the latitude and longitude coordinates of Tongor were given. "Find that area," she said firmly as she watched the holographic image play out. "If it's not in your memory bank, then find a map. Do it *now*."

"My God," Peacock murmured, his brown eyes wide. "This is unbelievable."

"To you, only two years have gone by. To us, hundreds of lifetimes worth. By the time this transmission reaches you the human race as you once knew it will either be victorious or extinct. I know not which. Only that it must be so…"

The transmission scrambled and somehow Alex knew that this time it wouldn't bounce back. A deafening silence filled Work Pod 3 as all assembled absorbed the information they'd just been given. It was long minutes before anyone moved.

As if they'd all lost the power of speech, the crew of the *Methuselah* stared at each other like deer caught in headlights. Out of all of the would-be scenarios concerning what Earth was liable to look like when they disembarked, no one had envisioned something like this in their worst nightmare.

Elinor's eyes were wild with fear. Peacock and John looked as though they might vomit. Vlad, Wolfgang, and Kyla looked faint.

"I think we better go see how much ammunition we have left for our weapons," Alex murmured, breaking the silence as she slowly rose to her feet. On the inside she was shaking like a leaf, but she knew she couldn't let her crew see that. Someone had to remain strong. As captain and commander, the job fell to her. "Let's go."

CHAPTER THREE

Akron. Based upon the latitude and longitude coordinates the Zutairan man had given them, it appeared that was where the final battle had taken place.

Of all the possible places for the most important and deciding war in the history of humankind to be fought, Armageddon had been fought in what was once Akron, Ohio. When the *Methuselah* had left Earth, such a scenario had been as unlikely as France taking over the world and emerging its only megapower. Both, however, had come to pass.

Alex lay naked on the satiny-soft bed in her private cabin, her legs spread wide and her eyes closed as Marax orally pleasured her. She could see the droid's tongue flicking below the triangle of blonde curls, his mouth latching on to her swollen clit.

Besides their ability to perform tireless manual labor, there was a reason human-looking droids were sent on missions with astronauts and this was it. That's why at least one male and one female droid were always present on missions expected to go beyond the two or three month stage.

She wasn't in the mood for a cold, emotionless fuck, she thought on a gasp. Her hard nipples stabbed upwards as climax loomed closer and closer. She fantasized about Robert, pretending it was her husband's mouth sucking vigorously on her clit instead of the emotionless droid's. It was so much easier to pretend during oral sex than intercourse. So much damned easier...

Alex came on a loud groan that reverberated throughout the cabin. Her thighs shook around Marax's head. "Oh Robert!" she groaned. "*Oh God.*"

Blood rushed to heat her face as her nipples stiffened impossibly more. She moaned as she rode out the wave of pleasure, having needed the release more than she could ever recall needing one.

"I was named Marax by my creator," the droid stoically reminded her as his face emerged from between her legs.

She closed her eyes again, hating how quickly the fantasy had been shattered.

"Not Robert. Dr. Robert Frazier was the name of your deceased husband. He died in the year—"

"Yes, I know."

Alex's cheeks went up in flames as she rolled over onto her belly. She knew it was long past time to let Robert go. He had been a good man, a good husband, and a good scientist. But he was dead. Fifteen hundred years dead and buried. It was time to let go.

The period for mourning had long since passed. Robert would have understood. She needed to concentrate all of her energies on keeping her crew alive when they reached Earth, not on raging against the fates for what could never again be.

"Would you like me to lie beside you while you sleep, Dr. Frazier?" Marax asked in a monotone.

Alex's nostrils flared at the injustice of it all. She missed passion and emotions and love—and the comfort of falling asleep in the arms of someone who *wanted* her to be there.

Let go, Alex, she told herself. Let Robbie go...

"Yes," she whispered, giving in to the momentary weakness, to the desire to have skin-to-skin contact. She deserved it, she supposed. Once they stepped foot off of the *Methuselah* there would be no room for indulging in weakness. She didn't know what her crew would be facing out there, only that it would take her full concentration and force of will.

"Yes," she repeated, her voice a murmur. "I'd like you to lie beside me."

* * * * *

"You belong to me, Alexandria," he quietly hissed. "Offer yourself to me. Beg for my seed."

"Never," she choked out, her heart pounding. Tied naked to the huge bed, her thighs spread wide open, she knew what was coming next. Her entire body shook, fear engulfing her.

She had gotten out of the cage, but she wanted freedom.

Where are my men? Where are you? Help me!

"Look at me."

Oh no—please! Not again. Not this again! She wouldn't look at him—at *it*. Not now. Not ever.

"Look at me."

Her nostrils flared at the angry, harsh command. *Never.*

A forked tongue snaked itself around either side of her clit. It began rubbing—slow, sensual movements that made her nipples jut up on a gasp.

"*Mmmm,*" he purred, the sound reverberating in the back of his throat. "I think I'll help myself to more of your cream..."

* * * * *

"Incoming debris. Incoming debris. Incoming debris..."

Phariz's warning sounded repeatedly over the intercom. Alex jumped out of bed, Marax forgotten as quickly as the droid always forgot her upon exiting her cabin.

Why do I keep dreaming about that…that – thing? Shaking off the last remnants of the nightmare she'd been subjected to while asleep, she threw on her uniform and raced down the north corridor toward Work Pod 1.

"Incoming debris. Incoming debris. Incoming debris…"

It was impossible to gauge the seriousness of the situation from the droid's tone of voice. Whether announcing the time of day on earth or the fact that the crew was facing death, her monotone was always the same.

"Incoming debris. Incoming debris. Incoming debris…"

"What do we got?" Alex shouted out to Peacock as she dashed toward where he was seated.

"Asteroids," Dr. Nielson answered for him since Lt. Williams was busy flying the spacecraft. John was standing behind Peacock, taking readings from over his shoulder. "And lots of them."

"Shit."

"You got that right," Peacock murmured as he maneuvered them through the asteroid belt. Sweat was breaking out all over his face. "This doesn't look good, Alex."

"John?" she asked as she fell into the seat next to him. "Talk to me, Dr. Nielson."

"Millions of pieces," he muttered. "Maybe even billions. They're big as hell, Alex. And they're moving at an astounding rate. I've never seen anything like this."

Apparently not, Alex thought, her heart rate picking up. This was the first time in two years Peacock had been obliged to steer the craft for reasons other than to practice so he could stay well-honed at the craft. The autopilot had been able to successfully maneuver them from all other potentially tricky spots.

"It's not natural," Vlad announced in a heavy Russian accent as he ran into Work Pod 1. His breathing was labored. "My readings show that this phenomenon is not the likely result of natural means."

Alex's face remained stoic, but her insides were screaming. "A nuclear explosion maybe? Like a war?"

"Da. Yes."

Alex's gaze locked with John's. "Fuck," he whispered.

Her thoughts exactly.

"How long ago?" Alex asked. "Any conjecture?"

"Elinor thinks roughly three hundred years in Earth time," Vlad announced as he scanned the technical reports he'd printed out back in Work Pod 2. "That would have made the year—let me do the math…"

Alex nodded. Her teeth sank down into her lower lip.

Vlad looked up. His eyes were wide. "2792," he said hoarsely.

The date of Armageddon.

Silence.

"What are we going to do, Alex?" John murmured.

Think, Alex, think...

"Keep us on course for Earth, Peacock," she whispered.

"There probably is no Earth left!" John growled as he surged to his feet. "You'll kill us all, commander!"

Alex's nostrils flared. "We're dead anyway if we don't return," she gritted out, surging to her feet. "Think rationally, doctor. This spacecraft is manned for two and a half years max. One way or another we could die. This, frightening as it is for all of us, is the only way we stand a chance."

John began to pace as he swore under his breath. He looked like a caged animal, his hands briskly running through his dark, wavy hair.

"You know she's correct," Vlad said quietly to John. His voice was firm if a bit shaky. "We can't survive without either refueling or decompressing. Check with Phariz on the probability if you so desire, but I'm willing to venture that the chance of surviving after decompressing on Earth is far greater than the chance of finding a space station that hasn't been blown to bits to refuel on."

"Fuck!" John swore, still pacing.

"Quiet," Peacock rumbled out, his eyes narrowed in concentration. "The noise is distracting."

An asteroid chunk the size of a small airplane struck the *Methuselah*, causing all but Peacock—who was harnessed into his chair—to fall to the ground. The lights flickered on and off and a sickening vacuum sound hiccupped in Work Pod 1 as the sensory doors sealed it off from the rest of the spacecraft.

"Elinor!" Vlad shouted, dragging himself up to his feet. "I need to get to Elinor!"

"It's too late!" John shouted back, tackling him. He wrestled Vlad to the floor, pinning him down. The big Russian fought back with everything he had in him, the loss of his wife making his eyes go wild and his voice guttural.

"Hold him down!" Alex yelled out to John. *And don't let him look up.*

Because if he looked up, she thought in horror, he'd be able to see the cameras that were visually relaying to Work Pod 1 what was happening to the rest of the *Methuselah*. Alex clamped a hand over her mouth while she watched a small hole in Work Pod 2 cause the entire chamber to explode...Elinor included.

Her heart thumping madly, Alex gritted her teeth as she pulled herself up to her feet. "Detach us from the main part of the craft!" she called out to

Peacock who was sweating in rivulets. She harnessed herself into the console chair next to him. "Do it—now! The others are dead. There is no time—do it!"

She could hear Vlad sobbing from behind her. Closing her eyes briefly, she took a calming breath. "Do it," she murmured. "Now."

Peacock nodded as he steered with one hand and reached for the correct button with the other. "You two harnessed, John?" he bellowed.

"Yeah!" John shouted back. "Do it, Peacock!"

A blink of an eye later, Work Pod 1 detached from what was left of the *Methuselah* and continued its rocky journey through the asteroid belt. The visual monitors aboard what was now *Methuselah II* showed the abandoned craft exploding before they scrambled and went black. Loud horns blazed throughout the work pod, the lights continuously blinking on and off.

Alex's gaze flew to the official Earth date and time monitor. *What the…?*

3999 A.D.

4982 A.D.

And counting.

"What the hell is going on?" she whispered, her eyes widening.

6821 A.D.

7039 A.D.

"John!" she shouted. "I need you over here as soon as possible!"

9975 A.D.

10,102 A.D.

She felt like she was going to be ill.

13,000 A.D.

"Please let this be wrong," Alex whispered. "Please let this be malfunctioning."

She cocked her head to look back at Vlad and John. Vlad was harnessed to John and John, teeth gritting and muscles bulging, was holding onto the reins of a workstation with his life. She could easily see how much strain his muscles were enduring for the skintight, black bodysuit he wore outlined that fact. Still, she knew the doctor well enough to realize they'd both be okay. Thank God.

"Vlad, get control of yourself and help John get you both up here. Now," Alex concluded shakily enough to warrant everyone's attention.

She was always stoic and in control. That she appeared to be just the opposite was apparently enough to get Vlad thinking rationally again. He pulled himself off of John and grabbed a hold of a strap dangling from a workstation.

Alex's head swiveled back around to view the date and time monitor.

30,010 A.D.

"What's going on?" Peacock quietly asked. He didn't glance away from the window viewing area.

She could see the muscle in his jaw tensing as he maneuvered them through a shower of asteroid chunks.

Alex used the back of her hand to swipe at the perspiration running down her brow. "Check the date and time monitor when you can afford to look at it," she murmured.

47,979 A.D.

"The date and time monitor? Why?"

56,809 A.D.

"Just do it," she whispered.

Peacock did. Alex could tell he wanted to do a double take, but he couldn't risk glancing away from the viewing area again. "Shit," he swore. "What the fuck is going on?"

"I don't know," she said as calmly as possible. "I really don't know."

700,888 A.D.

"What the hell has got you looking like that, Alex?" John called out, his teeth grinding together. He groaned as he pulled himself into the seat on the other side of her and strapped himself in.

A quick glance to the side confirmed that Vlad was still dazed, but okay. He'd managed to strap himself into the chair on the other side of Peacock.

"Alex?" Dr. Nielson prodded again when she didn't respond. His gaze flew to where hers seemed to be glued. "What is—holy shit! What the hell is going on?" he bellowed.

1,007,806 A.D.

"I don't know," Alex said unblinkingly. "I was hoping you would."

John fiddled with the computer console attached to the monitor. He cursed under his breath. "It's not malfunctioning," he rasped out. "The system looks to be online and working properly."

She nodded, but said nothing. Sweat gathered between her breasts, trickled down the sides of her face.

3,000,999 A.D.

"Earth—or at least I think it's Earth—is within our sights," Peacock announced.

They were approaching far too quickly. It had to be a phenomenon of the asteroids they'd encountered.

"Everyone prepare for an emergency landing," Alex concluded as the console she was working at confirmed Peacock's supposition. She took a deep breath as a groaning sound pummeled *Methuselah II*. It sounded as if the work pod was being grated against two asteroids. It sounded as if they were about to be smashed to bits.

"Everyone hold on!" Peacock shouted. "The entry is going to be rough!"

The lieutenant hadn't exaggerated. The spacecraft was bounced around so jarringly that Alex's teeth kept crunching together. She bit down—

hard—onto one of the straps securing her to keep her teeth from chipping out of her mouth.

3,702,999 A.D.

And counting.

"We're going through!" Peacock bellowed. "We going through and we're going down fast!"

4,878,999 A.D.

"What the hell?" John asked incredulously. "Why does the atmosphere look red?"

Alex didn't know so she didn't bother to answer.

7,221,999 A.D.

"We're in!" Peacock shouted. "I'm letting out the rotation wings."

The *Methuselah II* made one last hiccupping sound before its main engine went dead and its wings flew out.

"Aim for water," Alex murmured, the sensation of floating an almost-too-peaceful contrast to the previous bouncing around they'd done. She realized, however, that they weren't in the clear until they found water. "Assuming there is any down there."

"I can't visually confirm or deny that yet," Peacock muttered. "I'm trying. I'm—yes! Yes! There is water down there!"

"This is the first time NASA has been obliged to put the full transformation of a space vessel to the test," John said. "Here's hoping the submarine system works."

Alex blew out a breath. Like everyone else on board, her heart rate was far too high, her adrenaline pumping. "Kill the wings, Peacock. We have to hit the water like a cannonball for the submarine system to go on autopilot."

"I hope the water here runs deep enough," John mumbled.

"Me too," Alex whispered.

She held her breath as the *Methuselah II's* wings retracted and the vessel went plummeting from the sky at dead weight, descending so rapidly it made her brain ache. She closed her eyes and gritted her teeth, clamping a hand to her forehead.

"Here we go," Peacock drawled in a warning tone, causing her eyes to fly open. He engaged the protective shutters so that they closed over the window viewing area. It was extra reassurance that there would be no shattering of the tough see-through diamond barrier when they hit bottom. "Ten seconds to impact."

Before they knew what they'd done, the four warrior-scientists had clasped each other's hands. Even Vlad had returned from the land of the dead long enough to ascertain that his number might be up next.

"Five seconds to impact," Alex breathed out. "Four. Three. Two. One…"

A jarring crash-thud sounded throughout the work pod as the explorers held tighter to each other's hands. They had hit water. Now it was just a question of whether or not the body of water they'd landed in had been deep enough to sustain the crash without exploding the vessel.

Ten seconds went by. Twenty seconds.

The surviving crew let out a collective breath of relief. They had done it. Against all odds, they were alive.

"Good job, Peacock," Alex whispered. Her adrenaline was pumping and crashing so fast she felt nauseated. She imagined the remaining crew felt the same way. "Your flying saved us."

Peacock looked too shell-shocked to form words. Alex's forehead wrinkled as she regarded him. She watched him swallow roughly, his Adam's apple bobbing once in response. She raised an eyebrow.

"He's looking at the date and time monitor, Alex," John rasped out. "I think you better take a look too."

She stilled. She had momentarily forgotten about that.

Alex inhaled deeply and blew it out. She forced her gaze toward the monitor, not wanting to look but realizing that she had to.

Shit.

Alex's eyes widened from over the hand she'd unconsciously clamped over her mouth. Goose bumps formed on her arms as chills raced down her spine.

The monitor's final reading: 100,000,007 A.D.

Chapter Four

It was another ten minutes, ten excruciatingly surreal minutes of staring at the time and date monitor, before anybody moved, let alone spoke.

"One hundred million and seven," Vlad breathed out. "Surely this must be wrong—"

"No," Alex interrupted in a monotone that could have rivaled Phariz's. "It's not."

"Let me get this straight," Peacock said, his voice kept to a hush. He briskly rubbed the palms of his hands together. "We are the only survivors—not even the droids made it."

"Correct." She laid her head back on the console's chair with a sigh and stared at nothing.

"We crash-landed on Earth, but somehow managed to overshoot the landing by ninety-nine million, nine hundred and ninety-six thousand years, give or take a decade."

"Correct."

"We have no idea what's out there—hell, the air might not even be breathable or the water might be contaminated."

She sighed again. "Correct."

"We have whatever supplies were in this pod before we hit the asteroid belt, which amounts to all of a single change of uniform apiece and two days worth of food and water. Maybe some ammo if we're lucky."

"That about sums it up," she murmured, her eyes unblinking.

"I see." Peacock nodded. "And I'm the only one in here who thinks he might shit his pants?"

John snorted at that. "Not likely, bro."

"Nyet," Vlad muttered. "I think I've beat you to that one, comrade."

Alex shook her head slightly, finding her first smile. "You okay, Vlad?" she murmured.

He sighed, glancing away. He was silent for a moment and then, "Did she go quickly?" He looked back to Alex, his nostrils flaring. "Lie to me if you must."

"She went quickly." Alex locked eyes with the Russian. "And that's not a lie."

He nodded, glancing away again. "Then I will grieve for my Elinor once we're okay," he said quietly. "She would want me to make it. I know in my heart she would."

Just like Robert. Alex closed her eyes and took a deep breath. When she opened them again, she removed the harness straps securing her in and stood up. "Then let's make sure we survive."

"What in the hell are we gonna do?" Peacock asked. He unstrapped himself from the harness. "This is your area, Alex. Not mine. You're the expert at exploring alien terrain."

"Hey, this isn't alien," John teased. "We're home, buddy." He stretched his hands. "Out there is our beloved Earth." He raised an eyebrow. "Or is it New France?"

"As long as it isn't fucking mutant land, I don't give two shits." Peacock's lips puckered into a frown as he rose to his feet. "I'm here to tell you I've had one hell of a bad day. I'm in no mood to deal with a bunch of bitches who belong in a sideshow carnival."

Alex found her first chuckle. She walked to the other side of the pod and checked the munitions safe. "Well, here's one good thing. We've got ten small electrical bombs, six knives, six Laser-5 guns, and enough electrical current in reserve to blow up a large city."

"Excellent." John nodded. "And according to *Methuselah II*, the pod has almost breached the surface of the water. Another two minutes or so. Then we decompress for another fifteen."

"And then we go out there," Vlad muttered. He exchanged a wary glance with Alex. "Wherever and whatever *there* is."

Alex didn't say anything to the others, but she understood why Vlad was feeling so hesitant. She had the same niggling feeling in the pit of her stomach. She turned around and faced what was left of her crew. "I want us to make a pact. Right here. Right now."

That snagged everyone's attention. John's brow furrowed. "Sure, Alex. What's going on?"

"Maybe nothing." She sighed as she twisted her long blonde curls into a tight bun at the nape of her neck.

"But maybe something." This from Peacock. "I saw that weird look you and Vlad exchanged. I don't keep secrets from you, Al. Don't go keeping them from me."

"Okay, that I definitely don't like the sound of." John pinched the bridge of his nose. "Will one of you please enlighten me and the P-man here?"

Vlad frowned. "It's just that I keep thinking back to my undergraduate studies in Moscow."

"And?" John asked.

"And, well, a lot can happen in one hundred million years, comrades."

John raised an eyebrow.

"What Vlad is saying," Alex interrupted, "is this—if that genuinely was a nuclear explosion that rocked Earth back in the year 2792, we probably lost most, if not all, of humankind."

Vlad nodded. "In the twenty-second century, it was widely accepted by scientists that humans would probably not continue to evolve. At least not significantly." He gave them a quick lesson in biology. "Certain factors must be present for evolution to occur and chief amongst them is the necessity of having a breeding ground—space to evolve. This is why it was believed that city life made the continuing evolution of the human species an improbability. When we left Earth, there was no such thing as country life anymore. The entire world was too overpopulated for it."

"Too many people, too little breeding ground," Alex confirmed.

Vlad sighed. "But if a nuclear war killed off most of humanity…"

"Then what humans did manage to survive had the breeding ground necessary for evolution to resume." Alex's gaze flicked over her men. "Only we don't yet know if any humans survived. Maybe nobody survived." She took a deep breath and blew it out. "Or maybe," she said softly, "it was the opposing side that managed to live. And breed."

John and Peacock stilled.

Alex snorted. "Hence the uncomfortable glance between Vlad and me."

"So what you're saying," Peacock asked, having regained the power of speech, "is that if those mutated motherfuckers survived and made babies…" He shook his head. "They could be even stronger and deadlier than they were one hundred million years ago?"

"We just don't know, Peacock. We can't know until we get out there and do some looking around."

Alex nodded. "Which brings me back to my original statement. I want us to make a pact."

"A pact," John mumbled. "Right." He ran a hand over his stubbled jaw. "Well, let's make it then. What is it?"

Alex waited until all of the surviving crew was looking at her. "Our greatest chance of making it through whatever lies ahead is staying together. Nobody does anything stupid, nobody tries to be a hero. Got it?" When all three men nodded, she continued. "We have no idea what kind of a world we're about to step off into. It could be a peaceful, wonderful place or…"

"Or it could be hell on Earth," Peacock muttered. "Shit."

She inclined her head. "We just don't know," she murmured. "So let's make a pact that we stick together at all times. It doesn't take a genius to figure out that there's more safety in numbers." She narrowed her eyes at them, underlining her seriousness and how much thought she'd given the situation. "If for some unforeseen reason we get separated, we must promise that we will not stop searching until we're reunited or a corpse recovered. Agreed?"

They murmured their agreement, then stood there silently, nobody moving, as they stared at each other. A long, tense moment followed until Alex chuckled, piercing the quiet.

"There's something funny?" John inquired, a dark eyebrow raising.

She shrugged. "I'm probably being silly. I doubt anything could have survived a nuclear war as devastating as that one. Not even those mutants."

"True," Vlad slowly agreed. "Unless their genetic make-up became superhuman or something." His eyes narrowed as he considered the possibility. "But I doubt such a race could have sprung up in a single century, which was the period of time between the biological war between the USA and Japan and the rise of the mutated humans." He shook his head. "I don't know what was in those weapons but I doubt it could have been so powerful as that. If the humans died off in the nuclear war that followed, then the mutants probably did as well."

Alex inclined her head. "So we're probably being overly cautious here. Heaven only knows the worst discovery we might make out there is that the four of us are it. And since I think of the three of you as brothers, I guess that would mean the human race will definitely die out in our lifetime."

The four of them had a laugh over that. Alex grinned. "Unless there are droids out there that managed to survive, I suggest getting your hands in excellent condition." She winked. "You'll be using them a lot."

* * * * *

"Well, this is it." Alex took a deep breath and blew it out as she glanced up at the hatch. "John's readings came back fine, so we know the air is breathable and the water is drinkable. The chemical breakdown is a bit different than it was in our day, but there's nothing harmful in either." She glanced down at the others. "Unfortunately, that's all we know. I want everybody armed, Laser-5s on full charge. Are we ready?"

"Yeah, we're ready," Peacock confirmed as he stashed a knife into the leather strap he wore around his right thigh. "Let's do it, boss lady."

"John?"

"Ready, commander."

Alex nodded. "Open the hatch, Vlad."

Vlad muttered something in Russian under his breath as he reached for the button, then translated it into English. "Here goes nothing."

The sound of decompressing air hissed throughout *Methuselah II* as the hatch door opened. Because the craft had been built with the intention of returning to Earth via water, a ten-person life raft made of a nearly impenetrable synthetic material automatically shot out into the waters beside the work pod and ballooned up to its full length as soon as the door to *Methuselah II* had been opened. Still attached to the vessel, it wouldn't leave its host until the crew was ready for it to.

Alex's heart began beating rapidly, the thrill of discovery coursing through her blood. She couldn't stop the adrenaline rush, for it was part and parcel of the exploration process. That she was about to explore the world she'd once called home made no difference. That world had died out a hundred million years ago. In its wake was a place just as alien to her and the rest of the crew as any other uncharted planet.

"Here we go," she murmured as she climbed the rest of the way up the steel ladder. She stopped just shy of going through the portal and did one last weapons check. Patting herself down, she ascertained that her belt was on securely and that it contained her share of the goodies. A Laser-5 in one loop, two electrical bombs and assorted equipment in the pouch, a knife that emitted a deadly venom upon puncture in a second loop, and a pocketknife in a third.

She put the other Laser-5, the one in her hand, on full charge, held it above her head with both hands, and quietly made her way through the hatch door. Scurrying out onto the small deck that could hold no more than two people at a time, she held the Laser-5 out as she whirled around in a circle, the lightning fast move done so she could shoot at anything in the vicinity if she needed to.

Nothing, she thought, releasing a pent-up breath as she relaxed her trigger arm. Thank goodness for that.

Alex took an investigative look around. It was so black out that she couldn't register a thing. Clearly it was nighttime wherever they had landed. That seemed a bit odd since the date and time monitor had said they'd landed in the middle of the afternoon. Of course, she reminded herself, the date and time monitor had been set to central time, or what had been central time one hundred million years ago. Plus, they could have landed on the other side of the globe for all she knew.

She squinted her eyes as she tried to make heads or tails out of what the location they'd landed in looked like. Too dark. Far too dark. "Damn it."

"What is it?" she heard Peacock shout from below. "Alex, are you okay?"

"I'm fine," she said without glancing down. "Do we happen to have a lantern down there?"

"No. Why?"

She sighed. "Because it's so dark out I can't see a thing. We've got two choices," she said as she continued looking around. "Stay in the work pod until daylight and then paddle out, or try to paddle out of here now. I've got to warn you, though. If we choose the latter, we'll be paddling blindly. The dark is impenetrable. My eyes still haven't adjusted to it."

"I don't think we have a choice," John informed her as he climbed up the ladder rung. His head popped out of the hatch. "The further this vessel drifts, the worse the readings come back."

Alex turned to look at him. Her eyes narrowed. "What do you mean?"

"I mean that north equals good and south equals bad. The further south we drift, the more contaminated the water supply becomes. I'm picking up increasingly acidic levels. We need to paddle north. Now. At least we know that north equals uncontaminated water."

She nodded. "Let's do it then. Tell the others to follow you up."

Alex carefully made her way to the life raft and stepped into it. After confirming that it was working properly, she motioned for the others to follow suit. One by one they exited the hatch, scurried out onto the small deck, and then alighted into the raft. Once all four of them were safely inside of it, she handed the paddles to Vlad and Peacock.

"You two paddle," she instructed. "John, continue to take your readings." She pulled a pair of high-powered binoculars out of the pouch attached to her belt. "I'm going to see if I can make out any signs of land ahead."

All four of them went to work. Slowly but steadily they made their way in the opposite direction of the abandoned *Methuselah II*.

"Goddamn," Peacock muttered. "I sure wish we didn't have to paddle against the current. Can't anything go right today?"

"The current wants to take us south," Vlad explained when Alex and John looked at Peacock quizzically. "And we need to move north."

John nodded. "The readings come back better and better the further north we go." He frowned. "Something strange, though. The water really must have changed in a hundred million years. No matter how far north we go, it still doesn't have the chemical breakdown it should. There is a small level of acidic compound no matter what."

"It won't be drinkable?" Peacock asked on a grunt as he continued paddling against the current.

"I think it'll be drinkable," John conjectured. "It doesn't seem to have any more acid than an orange this far north."

"I see light!" Alex excitedly announced. "Just up ahead!" She lowered the binoculars and turned a bit to face her crew. "It looks red tinted. Just like you said the atmosphere looked when we first breached Earth, John."

He absently inclined his head, then continued to take readings. Hanging over the raft, his body stilled. "Uh, Alex…"

"Yeah?" She lifted the binoculars back up to her eyes and gazed around. There was something funny going on in her stomach, some weird sixth sense or something.

"Why is it that you can make out light coming up ahead, but we can't see any from where we're at?"

His statement nailed that funny feeling on the head. Her muscles tensed. Paddling around in what was presumably the ocean, they should have been able to make out light from any position. It was as if they weren't yet out in the open but would be soon.

Which could only mean that they were currently in an enclosed space.

"I don't know," she said slowly, lowering the binoculars. Something was wrong—very, very wrong. A feeling of panic began to engulf her, making her heart rate increase. "Paddle faster," she whispered. "A lot faster."

Peacock and Vlad began paddling as if their lives depended upon it.

A red-tinted light slowly began to penetrate the dark space. The further north the raft got, the more they could see. Alex squinted as she made out an odd shape coming up about a half mile out. She raised the binoculars, hoping to get a better look.

Her breathing stilled.

Oh. My. God.

"J-John," Alex stuttered out. She lowered the binoculars and turned to him wide-eyed. "Tell me if you see the same thing I do," she said hoarsely.

John's eyes had widened in reaction to hers. Without saying a word, he picked up the binoculars and—

"Jesus H. Christ."

"What?" Peacock shouted. "What the hell is going on?"

"Shh!" Alex chastised. "Lower your voice!" she said in a firm whisper.

Vlad's eyes rounded. "Tell us. Tell us now."

John lowered the binoculars. He cocked his head to regard Vlad and Peacock. "There's a big tooth up ahead," he breathed out. "A fucking tooth."

"A...tooth?" This from Peacock.

Alex took a deep breath. Her heart was beating so fast she could hear blood pounding in her ears. "Look over there," she rasped out, pointing to the left. "Look."

All eyes turned to where she was pointing. As the red-tinted light further penetrated the darkness, a wall slowly became visible. A wall that appeared to be made out of muscle. A wall that was contracting...

Breathing.

"Holy God," Peacock muttered, paddling faster. "What in the hell are we inside of?" His eyes looked wild, as wild with fear as Alex felt.

The tooth loomed closer. It was massively huge and yet only the top half was visible. The bottom was completely submerged in water.

"We're in some sort of sea creature," she breathed out. "It must have swallowed *Methuselah II* when we free-fell from the sky."

"I think it's sleeping," John said in a quiet voice. She could tell he was doing his best to contain his alarm. His eyes were as round as hers. "Let's make sure it stays that way," he murmured.

Alex forced her breathing to steady. *Do not panic. Do not panic!* "Look at how massive the mouth is. I can't see a beginning or an end to it. I only know it's a mouth because of the tooth."

"It has to have more than one tooth," Vlad announced in a forced hush. She could see how labored his breathing was becoming. "Which means the radius of its mouth doesn't bear thinking on."

"Calm down," Alex said to Vlad, forcing herself to do the same. "Your chest is heaving up and down. Calm it down now."

"There's a second tooth," John said quietly. "It's set approximately ten feet from the first tooth. There's a third one—another ten feet. This fucker," he shakily concluded, "is goddamn huge."

"But asleep," Alex reminded her crew. She was shaking like a leaf on the inside, but sounded surprisingly calm. "Otherwise its mouth wouldn't continuously be open."

"What kind of a sea creature sleeps with its mouth half in and half out of the water?" Peacock asked. The tight leash reining in his panic was growing more and more threadbare, she could tell. All of them were feeling the same way.

"It has to be bigger than a blue whale," Alex whispered. "With a body size like that it needs a lot of food. Maybe it skims the water for it while asleep," she said in a hopeful voice. She swallowed around the lump in her throat. "It has the incisors of a predator, though, so it probably hunts while awake."

"Fuck!"

"Keep it quiet, P-man," John murmured. "We all feel the same way, bro. Let's not wake sleeping beauty up, okay buddy?"

"Okay," he said quickly, his eyes wide but otherwise looking rational. Sweat covered his face, drenched the part of his uniform shielding his torso. "Okay."

"We're nearing the mouth," Alex whispered. "Paddle us dead center between the two teeth."

Peacock and Vlad immediately obeyed. They were trying to paddle as fast as possible without making too much noise. On one hand Alex realized that they wanted out and they wanted out now, just like her, but on the other hand they'd all be goners if they splashed around too much. A fact that had everyone's nerves on edge.

They immediately knew when they entered the mouth. Long rows of smaller, razor-sharp teeth jutted out from the top of the sickly enclosure. Bits of flesh from a recent kill dangled from the roots of each one. Alex swallowed roughly.

The secondary teeth weren't as big as the primary teeth, but just as deadly. If this thing woke up and closed its mouth before they got out, Alex thought, her stomach twisting into knots, they'd all be cut to ribbons.

"We're almost out," she murmured as the raft floated between the two huge incisor-like teeth. "Another thirty seconds and we'll be in the open waters."

Thirty seconds later, they were out. "Don't look back yet," Alex whispered as she held the Laser-5 in a ready-to-kill fashion. "Let's just keep moving."

The others had no idea what the predator looked like and, she thought, it was probably best if things stayed like that until they got further away. Otherwise, they'd all go into a panic. But, as if he couldn't help himself, Peacock braved a look over his shoulder once they got another twenty feet out. "Oh Jesus," he said quietly, but with panic clearly tinting the words. "Oh holy God, we've got to find land. We've got to find land!"

John lifted his gaze up to the creature—then probably wished he hadn't. "Oh my God," he said hoarsely, his chest heaving up and down. "We've got to get out of here."

The creature's skin was a shiny, latex-looking black that perfectly matched the uniforms of the crew. It possessed a serpentine head that was so massive in diameter as to be startling—easily bigger than a four-story house. If it was any indication as to the size of its cranium, the slit to each of its nostrils was longer than five people together, one piled atop the other. If this thing woke up, they had no hope of survival.

Alex realized that she was grasping the Laser-5 far too tightly between her palms. She relaxed her hold just a bit, preparing to use the weapon should the smallest sound or movement come from the creature. She refused to consider the possibility that a Laser-5 might not wield enough juice to kill something of such massive proportions. Her heart was already beating far too fast—she didn't need to add to it by considering the grisly possibilities.

"Are there extra oars?" she breathed out, her gaze mesmerized by the sight of the huge thing. She couldn't seem to look away from it. "John and I can help paddle."

"Nyet," Vlad grimly answered. He squeezed his eyes shut just before his blond crew-cut was showered by a spray of water caused by a gust the creature's nostrils made on an exhale.

"Just go as fast as you can now," Alex ordered. "Paddle us fast."

"There's land!" John announced, his voice hopeful but hushed. "Paddle northwest!"

Alex turned her head in the direction John was pointing. Her eyes widened, both in disbelief of what she was seeing and awe.

The mountainous terrain approximately two miles out was obsidian in appearance and had a bizarre jagged structure. It looked more like a felled meteor than a mountain range, but then this Earth was not the planet it had once been. The Martian red sky attested to that fact as easily as the glossy black mountains did. The gargantuan predator they were steadily veering away from served as another, deadlier, reminder.

Don't think about that — don't think about that…

Off in the distance, curls of smoke rose up from all over the mountain range. Of human invention or natural means she couldn't tell, but from the rather steady formation of the smoke curls it was probably the latter. Pools of lava maybe. Or boiling oil perhaps.

Fifteen minutes later they'd paddled close enough for Alex to make out that the eerie mountain range had a metallic appearance, which probably meant the composite of it was more iron ore than dirt.

She turned her head and braved a look back at the water beast. *Still asleep*, she thought, nibbling on her lower lip. *Please stay that way.* They were well away from the sea creature now, but not yet close enough to land to escape if it was to awaken. She stared at the closed eye she could see from her vantage point, as if transfixed by it, as if willing it to stay closed.

We didn't make it this far to be snake food. Stay asleep you bastard.

Alex kept up her vigil for the next twenty minutes. The raft was almost to land. Close, so damn close...

Stay asleep. Stay asl —

The eye flew open.

Alex's breath caught in the back of her throat. Her wide, light green eyes made contact with the diamond-shaped iris of a massive silver one. "Paddle faster!" she ordered, her heart rate climbing. "Paddle faster!"

John's head swiveled around to the side. His gaze rounded. "Holy mother — faster!" he bellowed out to Vlad and Peacock. "It woke up! Move faster!"

It knew they were there.

Alex watched in surreal horror as the sea creature closed its gaping jaws with a sickening moaning sound and reared its gargantuan head. Its fangs bared, it rose up from the water at least fifty feet before a high-pitched keening sound erupted from its throat.

Sleeping beauty had awoken. And she wanted to hunt.

Alex detonated the Laser-5 without hesitation, firing a series of electrical pulses at the mammoth beast that would have instantaneously sizzled a lesser opponent to a crisp. "Shit!" she yelled, as she reached for one of the two electrical bombs in the pouch on her belt. "The Laser-5 isn't even fazing the thing!"

John added his firepower into the mix. He detonated a series of electrical pulses, aiming for the vulnerable throat. The sea creature moaned as if in pain—or pissed—but otherwise emerged unscathed. The visible part of its long, snake-like body began moving toward the life raft at an alarming speed.

"Aim for the eye!" Alex yelled out to John as she fiddled with the timer on the first electrical bomb. "Maybe that will stun it!"

"I can't get it in my sights! It's—goddamn it—paddle faster!"

Alex broke out into a cold sweat as the black sea creature drew frighteningly closer. She could tell by the way it was rearing up that it was preparing to drop its gargantuan head into the water as fast, and with as much deadly force, as its bodyweight could muster.

Think, damn it! Think!

If it dropped its head this close to them using all of its might, the raft would be ripped to pieces by the resulting tidal wave. If they weren't killed by the impact outright, their bodies would scatter overboard—and they'd be eaten alive.

Think!

Alex set the electrical bomb to detonate in thirty seconds, preparing to hurl it at the beast. Thinking quickly, she recalled that *Methuselah II* had probably been swallowed as it free-fell from the sky.

This is your one and only chance, Commander Frazier. Don't fuck it up...

Praying that her hunch was right and that the sea creature's innate reflex would be to open its gaping jaws for anything it espied in its peripheral vision, she threw the bomb as high into the air as she could, aiming toward the mammoth serpent's eye. She smiled slightly, her breath shuddering, when the creature swallowed the electrical bomb whole.

Twenty seconds to detonation.

Please have enough juice.

"Don't tell me what's happening!" Peacock shouted as he and Vlad continued to paddle with the full force of their combined musculatures. Their jaws were clenched, their vein-roped arms bulging, as they gave it everything they had in them. "I don't want to know!"

As if in slow motion, Alex watched in horror as the creature's head came barreling down towards the water. *We're going to die*, she thought. *We're going to —*

John's Laser-5 aimed true, piercing the beast's retina. The sea creature half-bellowed and half-hissed as its head stopped in midair, its neck visibly recoiling from the assault. "Die, fucker!" John raged.

It fell backward, submerging into the water, knocking its upper length back a solid hundred feet. The resulting current jarred the raft twenty feet in the opposite direction, closer to land. John fell overboard, the only one of the four to have been standing at impact.

"John!"

Ten seconds to detonation.

Please, God, please…

The beast's head rose up once more, its hideous jaws gaping. Now blind in one eye, the water serpent zigzagged its head around in a series of jarring motions as if trying to locate something…or someone.

Five seconds to detonation.

Zeroing in on its prey with its remaining eye, the creature was interested in making a meal of the one who had injured it—John. John had managed to drag his injured body up to the shoreline since he'd been thrown so near to land, but he was still too close to the water's edge. The horrific realization that the beast could think at a level advanced enough to understand vengeance became crystal clear to Alex at the precise moment it made a hissing sound and began dropping its head down toward the felled scientist.

"Nooo!" Alex raised her Laser-5 and targeted the second eye. The creature bellowed at contact, its second retina sizzled. It recoiled again, falling backwards into the waters at the precise moment the electrical bomb detonated.

The resulting boom pummeled the water from below, sending the raft and its remaining crew hurling in random directions. Alex went numb as she hit the frigid black water, gasping when she surfaced.

She wasn't above water for more than five seconds when a chunk of serpent blubber rained down on top of her, forcing her below the surface and trapping her beneath it. She tried not to panic, but didn't succeed. Her eyes bulged from beneath the frigid water as her body madly flailed about, looking for escape but finding none. She clawed at the blubber, flopping around like a fish on a boat.

Somebody help me! Somebody —

A knife shot down from the middle of the blubber, piercing and slicing it. A hand wrapped around her hair and began pulling her up through the resulting hole. The pain to her skull was searing, but welcomed.

Alex gasped for air the second she breached the surface. Wheezing, she clutched onto Peacock for dear life as he bodily pulled her on top of the piece of carcass that had damn near killed her. "You saved," she panted out, "my life."

"And you saved all of ours," Peacock muttered. "Let's get the hell off this thing."

Two minutes later, Alex and Peacock joined Vlad and John on the iron-hard metallic shore. Alex motioned to John who was having his arm tended to by Vlad. "Are you okay?" she rasped out, still struggling to regain her breath.

John nodded. "My left arm suffered a mild sprain, commander, but otherwise I'm in tip-top shape." He winked. "Thanks for saving my ass out there."

She would have responded to that, but the sound of clanging weapons took her by surprise. Alex glanced up and, still panting, swore under her breath.

Her crew had been surrounded. This time by what appeared to be humans, or human-like beings. She hoped the former.

The primitively dressed group of ten, Alex noted, looked prepared to kill her and the crew where they stood if they warranted it as necessary. She considered going for her Laser-5 but discarded the idea. She had no idea how quick the reflexes of these fighters would prove to be and conceded that this might not be the opportune time to find out. She could always save that surprise for later. Her crew was too weak from the last skirmish to effectively fight back.

Hoping some things had managed to survive one hundred million years of evolution, Alex raised her arms in what she hoped to be the age-old sign of surrender.

CHAPTER FIVE

The ten humans surrounding them were dressed in nothing but loincloths and boots, both of which looked to be made out of some odd type of lizard skin. They were all a bit taller than what had been considered normal in the crew's day, the males roughly six and a half feet in height and heavily muscled, the sole female roughly six feet and although not as big, just as sturdy-looking.

Alex clutched the second Laser-5 in her grasp without removing it from her belt, the first one having been lost in the waters. She didn't want to use the weapon unless necessary, and her gut instinct told her it wouldn't be necessary if she cooperated. Sometimes instinct was all a person had to go on. She offered no protest when the female walked up to her and began bodily inspecting her.

The female was dark-haired, tall, and muscular, bringing to mind a fabled Amazonian warrior. She wore a loincloth and boots like her male counterparts, but her loincloth looked to be made of a finer, less coarse material than the males'. It was tied off on one hip in a knot and skirted to the side, the cloth concealing her buttocks instead of her mons — whether purposefully symbolic of female authority or simply indicative of the fact that nobody here thought female nudity dirty or odd, Alex didn't know.

The female's breasts were unbound, naked for anyone to see. None of her men seemed to care, though Alex's own crew was uncomfortably shifting back and forth on their feet, trying not to stare at her jutting nipples and the black triangle of hair between her thighs.

Metallic obsidian bangles clasped both of the female's biceps in a distinctly Cleopatra fashion. She wielded an odd weapon in one hand and painfully snapped Alex's head back by the hair with the other one. The leader was strong—very strong.

Alex prepared to pull out the Laser-5, but didn't when she realized that the female was merely looking into her eyes. When the leader was satisfied with whatever it was she did or didn't see there, she released her hair and muttered something in a strange tongue to her comrades.

Alex opened her mouth to speak, but was forestalled when the female began inspecting her teeth. Wide-eyed, and uncertain what to make of the poking and prodding, she again offered the female no resistance. The woman poked at her incisors, looking around for—something—then lowered her hand. As if mesmerized by the color of Alex's hair, golden blonde being an apparent anomaly here, she ran her fingers through it, then over the blonde line of her eyebrows.

The males of the clan treated Alex's crew to the same inspection of eyes and teeth. When all four of them had apparently checked out okay, the female — who Alex had rightly assumed to be the leader — inclined her head. It was not lost on the commander that this leader didn't so much as deign to speak to any of the males in Alex's party. Only to the other female...herself.

"Mali zynoot Fija," the serious-faced woman said. "K'yat zynoot?" She lowered her hand from Alex's face and waited for a response.

Alex glanced back at her crew and then to the leader of this band of humans. She shrugged her shoulders, hoping the alpha female understood the meaning of the gesture. "I do not understand what you are saying," Alex said slowly, over-enunciating each word.

The leader frowned. She looked Alex over as if trying to figure her out. Eventually she rumbled out an order to the males of her little band then walked away, dismissing Alex and her crew.

When the survivors of the *Methuselah* were roughly grabbed by the backs of their necks and forced to follow behind the female leader, Alex could only assume the males of the guard had been ordered to round the strangers up.

Alex shared a meaningful glance with Peacock, a look that clearly said — one false move by these people and we kill them all.

* * * * *

They were steered into the metallic mountains, a three-hour trek that was exhausting in the extreme to a group of people who had just finished crash-landing on Earth only to follow that experience up by fighting off a gargantuan-sized water predator. Nevertheless, the surviving crew of the *Methuselah* remained alert, their eyes trained on their captors, their hands ready to draw their weapons.

Alex hoped it didn't come to that. She had spent the last three hours studying the female leader and liked what she saw. Although the Amazon had a pompous air of superiority about her, she genuinely seemed to care for the welfare of those under her in rank. Even her prisoners. She stopped without complaint and allowed everyone to take a breather when needed. She slowed down her gait for the tired crew rather than using physical threats to cajole them into moving faster to keep up with her. All signs of an honorable leader to Alex's way of thinking.

By the time the group was led through a small break in the metallic mountainside and shuffled down a dimly lit path, hunger pangs were knotting in Alex's belly. Her crew was led into a small cavern that resembled a medieval torture chamber with its shackles, iron pokers, and prods—not to mention the noticeable bloodstains on the walls.

She could only assume this was where she and her crew would be interrogated before being taken further into the belly of the metallic mountain—or wherever it was this tribe's people called home.

For reasons unknown, probably instinct, the impending interrogation didn't worry Alex. She only prayed her intuition was dead-on where the female leader was concerned.

If not, she thought, her hand on her Laser-5, the interrogation would turn ugly.

* * * * *

Peacock bellowed in pain and outrage as the men subduing him forcibly opened his mouth and shoved some horrid looking needle-like mechanism between two of his teeth. When they detonated the object, he began to convulse. The Amazon, apparently aware of the fact that Alex was about to draw a weapon, lifted a negligent hand and shook her head as if to say, *this is not harming your male, just watch.*

Alex's nostrils flared as she regarded the woman. Holding her stare in a show of challenge, she eventually inclined her head, relenting.

When the men let go of Peacock, they didn't back up in time. With a growl, he kicked two of them squarely in the jaw, his nostrils flaring, his eyes narrowed. When he surged up to his feet, he cold-cocked a third male with his fist, causing the fighter to plummet to the hard metallic ground.

The Amazon found Peacock's show of brute strength funny—or maybe appealing. The leader threw back her head and laughed, inducing the males of her band to stare at her strangely. This only made the Amazon laugh harder. Alex sighed, shaking her head.

"What the fuck was that for?" Lt. Williams—Peacock—bellowed to the Amazon. She answered him back, causing him to frown. "And just why am I not worthy of questioning you? Because I have a dick! Now wait a minute, sister—" Peacock stopped mid-tirade. His eyes widened in comprehension at the same time Alex's did.

"They injected some sort of translation device into you," Alex whispered. She shared an excited glance with John and Vlad. "Go on," she prodded, "your turns."

"No way," Vlad said, his hand slashing definitively through the air. "How do we know what effect this mechanism will have in a year, or even in an hour? For all we know the injection could cause us to grow scales. Or breasts!"

John visibly shuddered.

"Oh my God," Peacock moaned as he clamped a hand to his forehead. Thinking that statement over, he grabbed his very masculine pecs, his face clearly relieved when he failed to find anything new and noteworthy there.

Alex frowned. Farfetched as it sounded, Vlad had a point. Damn it! How could she have been stupid enough to allow Peacock to undergo that procedure without proof that it wasn't deadly? Her nostrils flaring, mostly at her own stupidity, she drew her Laser-5...and trained it on the Amazon. "You. Now. Show me it won't hurt my men. *Now*."

Peacock spoke to the Amazon, translating Alex's words to her. With a martyr's sigh and a slight shake to her head, the leader stoically sat down on the lizard-skin chair and offered no resistance as the same injection was then doled out to her. Peacock frowned when she failed to elicit even a tiny whimper in response to the painful procedure. Alex hid a smile.

Turning to face Vlad and John, Alex lifted an eyebrow. "Convinced?"

They muttered their yeas and took their turns being injected.

When it was Alex's turn to be injected, she fell into the lizard-skin chair, determined to remain just as stoic as the Amazon had. She needed to establish that she, too, was an alpha female here — clearly such a thing counted in this world.

Begin as you mean to go on. Establish your authority and dominance.

The Amazon nodded her respect when Alex underwent the painful procedure without so much as blinking. She stared at the leader the entire time, their gazes locked as if in challenge. By the time the injection was over and the bizarre, and admittedly advanced, translation device had lodged itself in her brain, Alex felt dizzy enough to pass out. She shook it off, standing up.

"So," the Amazon said, looking Alex up and down. "I will say to you again what I said to you three hours ago. My name is Fija. What is your name?"

She blinked. "Alex," she answered, in more awe than she cared to admit of the translation device. The Amazon was speaking in her own tongue, yet Alex's brain translated her words as if they'd been spoken in English. "Dr. Alexandria Frazier, Commander and Captain of the *Methuselah*."

The Amazon threw her head back and laughed. The men of her tribe followed on her heels, chuckling. Alex shared a perplexed look with her crew.

"Oh are you now, little warrior?" The Amazon grinned. "You are the fabled Alexandria the Great, eh? Alexandria the Great as foretold by the prophets. Come to set us free?" She shook her head at her men, still grinning. The males of her tribe shared another chuckle with their leader. She glanced back to Alex. "Don't you think you're a bit short to be a prophesized legend, little warrior?"

"I don't know what in the hell you're talking about, but I *am* Dr. Alexandria Frazier." Alex frowned. "And I'm not short. You are just exceedingly tall."

"Hmm."

"Look," Alex said, exasperated. She glared at the six-foot tall, all but naked female. "I don't particularly care if you believe me or not. Maybe I share the same name as the woman you spoke of. Whatever. All I do care about is finding out where the hell I am. And getting some food and water for my men and me since ours was lost in the ocean." She glanced at her crew, all of who looked as parched and hungry as she was. "And not necessarily in that order."

"You certainly have the manners of a warrior-queen," the Amazon muttered. She raised an eyebrow as she carefully looked Alex up and down. "Come. I will feed you and your males." The two leaders locked gazes. "And then we will talk."

CHAPTER SIX

"*Your* males," John muttered under his breath as they sat around the campfire finishing their meal of unleavened bread and roasted fish tongue. The crew of the *Methuselah* had been given its privacy while eating, the four of them a few feet away from the rest of the group. The meal was disgusting but it was all they had. "She keeps calling us that. The woman talks about men like chattel. I don't like it."

Alex didn't know what to say to that. The longer she talked to Fija, the more she got the feeling that Earth in 100,000,007 A.D. was a matriarchal place all over. Not at all the male-dominated Earth she and her crew had heralded from. In Alex's world, her honored position in life had been a rarity. In this world, it was the accepted norm for a female.

"I don't either." Peacock frowned. "Next thing you know that lady will have us pushing the vacuum and wearing ribbons in our hair."

"Da," Vlad grimly agreed. "I do not like this place."

Alex frowned at all of them. "Well now you know how I felt one hundred million years ago."

"Oh come on, Al!" Peacock shook his head. "It was never this bad." His forehead wrinkled. "Was it?"

She sighed. "It doesn't matter. The point is we have no idea where we are and what we plan to do from here. We have no home, and in so far as I can tell, no purpose here either. We need to come up with a game plan. Until then, this is it fellas." She raised an eyebrow. "So could you three please quit walking around with those woe-is-me expressions on and at least *try* to get along with Fija and her men?"

"When in Rome?" John asked, an enigmatic twinkle in his eye.

"Exactly," Alex agreed on a nod. "When in Rome, do as the Romans."

Peacock wiggled his eyebrows at her. "A great plan, boss lady." His grin was lethal. "Say, have a look at what the Romans are doing right now." He used his eyebrows to gesture over her shoulder.

Alex cocked her head, turning around just a bit so she could see what was causing her crew to quietly chuckle. Her eyes rounding, she could only gawk at the sight that greeted her.

"Suck on my pussy, unworthy beast," Fija instructed a male called Daab. Lying back on her elbows, the warrior woman's legs were spread wide apart while three of her entourage serviced her. The males were rubbing all over her body, caressing and fondling her intimately.

"Did you hear what she called that Daab dude?" Alex heard Peacock mutter to John and Vlad. "Unworthy beast. Ain't that some shit."

Alex barely spared Peacock a glance before turning back to watch the foursome unfold. She was mesmerized by the sight of it, having never witnessed such a decadent display of sexuality anywhere except in the movies. To that group of humans, sexuality looked as natural and desirable as it was supposed to be, free of all the religious and moral sanctions that had been placed on it so many millions of years ago.

The large, muscular male called Daab removed his fingers from the folds of Fija's wet vagina. Diving between her thighs, he replaced his hand with his face. His tongue snaked out and flicked repeatedly at the leader's swollen clit, making her hiss.

A second male's tongue darted out and found one of her hard, jutting nipples. He latched onto it with his mouth and sucked, his hand caressing one of her thighs as he did so. A third male latched onto Fija's other nipple, his tongue curling around the bud and suckling it hard.

Fija's hips bucked up, the pleasure she was feeing obvious. Daab chose that moment to stop flicking at her clit and to suction it into his mouth instead. Her dark eyes closed on a gasp as Daab vigorously sucked. She moaned, her head lulling back against a fourth male who did nothing but tenderly run his fingers along the sides of his leader's face.

"Harder," Fija gritted out without opening her eyes. "Suck on my pussy harder."

Daab must have obeyed for the leader was gasping and groaning within seconds. Alex chewed on her bottom lip as she watched Fija's hips rear up in a show of ecstasy. Arousal Alex'd never admit to in a million years—or one hundred million years—knotted in her belly from merely watching.

Fija's body began to convulse—violently. The males at her nipples sucked impossibly harder, evident by the further concaving of their cheeks. Daab nuzzled her clit like the beast she'd called him, a small growl erupting from his throat.

She came on a loud moan that echoed throughout the cavern, her entire body shaking and convulsing. Alex watched with more fascination than she cared to feel, idly wondering what it must feel like to be Fija in that moment.

Not that she'd ever allow her own crew to touch her like that. No way.

"So Al," she heard Peacock whisper in a teasing voice. "Let's go back to this whole when in Rome thing you were briefing us on."

Alex turned around and frowned at him.

"What?" John asked, feigning surprise. "We only want to be worthy beasts instead of unworthy ones."

Vlad's grin was so wide she could see the gleam of his white teeth. A rarity indeed for the stoic Russian never smiled.

"Oh you guys are just soooo funny." She glared daggers at all of them. "I'm afraid we'll be skipping that part of the tour of Rome."

John looked as though he wanted to tease her some more, but stopped, glancing up instead. Alex turned around, rightly assuming that they had company. She stood up, preparing to see what Fija wanted.

"So," the Amazon said. "I have shown you a glimpse of what my males can do." She locked gazes with Alex, never once deigning to so much as glance at the *Methuselah*'s surviving male crew. "I will trade you all three of them for your black-skinned male of the foul temper."

Now this was just too funny. Bemused, Alex looked to Peacock. For once the perfect features of his face and body had turned out to be a hindrance instead of a help. His expression was reminiscent of a deer that had been caught in headlights.

"Hell noooo!" Peacock bellowed, his anger at last piercing the quiet that had fallen. John and Vlad were snickering behind their hands. "Uh-uh. No way. No. That's my final word." He crossed his arms over his chest and glowered at the woman who wanted to buy him.

Said woman was not impressed. In fact, she never looked away from Alex, so she wasn't even aware of the fact that she was being glowered at.

Alex absently scratched her head, uncertain as to how she should proceed. Hundreds of would-be scenarios along with how to effectively deal with them had popped up over the course of her NASA training, but this had not been among them.

"Fija…" she began. Good lord, what could she say? She sighed. "My, uh, beasts are meaningful to me." She glanced over to Peacock whose nostrils were flaring then back to the Amazon. "I will not barter any of them."

Fija inclined her head. "If you change your mind, I should like you to remember my desire to own the feisty one."

"I will." She hesitated. "Thanks for the offer."

Apparently Alex had said the right thing, for the Amazon gave her a small smile. She looked Alex up and down, then raised that eyebrow of hers again. "Let us talk in private away from the ears of the gentle-minded, eh, little warrior?"

Alex turned to her crew and grinned. They merely frowned.

Gentle-minded, indeed. Fija might as well have referred to men as pathetic, weak vessels possessing no intelligence whatsoever.

She looked back to the Amazon and nodded. "Yes. Let's go talk." And then she threw out over her shoulder as they strolled into a nearby cavern, "far away from the ears of the *gentle*-minded."

The sound of her crew mumbling under their breath brought a smile to Alex's full lips. Heh heh.

* * * * *

Alex sighed as she took a seat on a nearby clump of reddish dirt. Thankfully, there was some sort of a soil base in this world, even if it was a peculiar one. Then again, she had known there would be at least some manner of soil and plant life down here from the moment John's readings had ascertained the air was breathable. Sustainable oxygen levels couldn't have been emitted without those two things in place. At least not by any means known to her and the crew.

"So that's what happened," Alex concluded, her eyes finding the Amazon's. Her gaze absently flicked over the female's bared breasts before returning to her face. "I thought about making up a story to try and appease you, but what's the point? Either you will believe me or you won't. The particulars don't matter."

The Amazon wore her trademark frown, her eyes narrowed thoughtfully. Alex bit into her lip, wondering what the other woman was thinking. She knew the story of the *Methuselah* would sound incredulous to her—perhaps too incredulous—had their roles here been reversed.

"Well?" Alex quietly asked.

"Well," Fija said cautiously, "let us just say I will jump to no conclusions and will reserve judgment for another place and time."

Alex frowned. "I guess that's the most I can ask for," she muttered.

The Amazon looked amused. She stood up and nodded. "Yes, little warrior, it is."

Alex sighed as she surged to her feet. "Why do you keep calling me that?"

Fija ignored her. "A bit of advice if you desire it."

Alex quirked an eyebrow but said nothing.

"Tell no other Takuri your tale. Not yet. It sounds...err...well, let us just say not many are so open-minded as me."

"Takuri?" Alex asked, puzzled.

Fija scanned her gaze. "You don't know what a—?" She blinked. "That's right. You're one hundred million years old," she said drolly. "Older even than the dead prophets. How could I forget."

Alex's jaw clenched. "I am not lying," she bit out. She rubbed her temples, weariness from the last several hours at last getting to her. "Never mind. What is a Takuri?"

"A rebel, little warrior," Fija murmured. "A human."

"A rebel," Alex whispered. She swallowed past the lump in her throat. "Care to enlighten me on what we humans are rebelling against?" She prayed it wasn't who—or what—she thought.

Fija sighed like a martyr. "If your tale is true, I must say I find it aggravating to converse with a one hundred million year old female. You behave like a male, a simpleton."

Alex's nostrils flared. "Those are fighting words, sister."

Fija threw her head back and laughed. "You are so short I need only pick you up by the scruff of the neck and hold you away from my body while you throw your fit of temper."

Alex couldn't help but to grin at that mental image. "Shut up," she said half-heartedly.

Fija's lighthearted smile turned into a serious expression. "We fight the Xandi, little warrior. They are evolved of the predator people. Our natural-born enemy."

A chill of awareness slowly trickled down Alex's spine. "I trust you'll debrief me more on these…things…as our trek to your camp continues?"

The Amazon's eyes narrowed appreciatively. "Things. A good word. Or demons. And yes, I will debrief you. But the night comes upon us soon, so for now we must go."

A certain déjà vu knotted in Alex's belly at Fija's use of the word demon. Now why did that trigger a memory?

"But first we needs get you changed into attire befitting a warrior that we might continue on our journey." She frowned. "You look as solemn and weak as a Priestess of the Temple wearing that pitiful frock."

That snagged Alex's attention. She frowned back. "What sort of attire are you—oh no!" she said, shaking her head. "No way am I walking around like you half-naked!"

Fija grunted. "You are strange to me."

"Strange but clothed!"

The Amazon shook her head. "Survival in this world is for the strongest of women and the males they offer their protection to. Do you think any will take you serious, so short as you are, when you can't even dress the part of a warrior?"

"Fija..." Alex said on a sigh.

"I cannot understand this modesty of body, but wear the body-plate of a warrior if it makes you feel less...whatever."

"Body-plate?" Alex asked hesitantly.

"It's what we wear in battle. A body shield." Fija snorted and shook her head. "The women of the clans will be curious as to why you have donned the dress of a female headed to battle. Then again, maybe such a ferocious appearance will make up for your small stature."

Alex grunted at that. She'd take what she could get. "All right. Fine," she relented, realizing she didn't have much of a choice. "I'll take the body-plate."

The Amazon inclined her head. "Wait here while I fetch one you can borrow." She began to walk from the cavern, then stopped abruptly and cocked her head to face Alex. "One more thing, little warrior."

"Yes?"

"When we come into contact with other Takuri, tell none of them your tale. Or your name."

Alex's eyebrows drew together curiously. "Okay. But why?"

Fija smiled without humor. "Because like as not they will accuse you of heresy and offer you to the xandor beast as sacrifice to the gods."

Alex blinked. She wasn't following the thread of the conversation. Nor did she know what a xandor beast was. "I don't understand…"

"You claim to be a woman foretold by the prophets."

"I never claimed—"

"Claiming as much is akin to claiming to be one of the very gods."

Alex's nostrils flared. "I said I never claimed—"

"Yes. You do," Fija said softly. "Tell them your name is Alex and tell them no more."

Alex sighed. "Or they'll kill me?"

Fija nodded. Her gaze locked with Alex's. "I do not know that I believe you. But I do know this—I don't want you dead before I decide if I believe you or not."

Alex snorted at that. "Gee, thanks for the honesty. At least I always know where I stand with you."

The Amazon's smile came slowly. "Quite welcome."

* * * * *

John whimpered. Peacock's mouth dropped open. Vlad's breathing was so still that he looked like the tin man from *The Wizard of Oz* after the snowfall had frozen him.

Alex's nostrils flared. "It's the dress of a warrior headed to battle," she gritted out. "Unless you want me to look like a pansy and watch the three of you get sold off right from under my nose, I suggest you stop staring and get used to it."

Peacock's mouth worked up and down but nothing came out.

John blew out a breath. "No, Al, we don't want you to look like a pussy—I mean pansy!" he quickly corrected when she glowered at him.

Vlad coughed into his hand and glanced away.

Alex frowned. The outfit was awful and she knew it. She looked like the result of a skirmish between Ben-Hur and a pleasure droid. So much for the brief flicker of hope she'd entertained that a body-plate might actually cover her body and allow for modesty. The *taku*, as Fija had called it when handing it over, was embarrassingly obscene. Still, it beat the hell out of walking around with all of her intimate parts bared to the world.

A see-through, clingy black gauze material shrouded Alex's body from neck to toe. Two unforgivingly tough silver metallic cups encased her breasts over the gauze, but managed to show off more than they concealed. A metallic g-string-like thing covered her lower half—barely—and was made of the same impenetrable material as the breast cups. A pair of metallic knee-high combat boots and a weapons-belt similar to her own finished off the "body" part of the body-plate.

Yet somehow the worst aspect of the entire ridiculous outfit, she conceded, was the outlandish helmet she'd been given to wear on her head. Where the body portion didn't offer enough protection to her way of thinking, the head portion offered far too much. She felt like a moron with a gigantic cone sitting on her head, her blonde hair coming out of a hole at the apex of it and flowing down around her shoulders.

Good Lord, what a hat. She looked like the Grand Poobah of the Slut People, she thought grimly.

"Are you finished staring?" Alex ground out to her crew, her eyes narrowed. "Or should I sell you three already?"

"Let us be gone," Fija loudly intoned from across the makeshift camp, interrupting the dressing down. "We've three hours of trekking left to us before we reach the Takuri stronghold." Her males immediately took to their feet, preparing to leave. "The night comes soon."

Alex raised an eyebrow as she watched the Amazon pick up her weapons and secure them to her body. She wondered why the night mattered so greatly to Fija. That was the second time she'd mentioned it. It was a question she had a feeling needed an answer, but one she also sensed would have to wait. For now, they just needed to get moving.

"I'm sorry if we made you feel like an idiot," John begrudgingly muttered, snagging Alex's attention. He wasn't one for apologies, but it sounded sincere, if a bit gruff. "That was wrong."

"Same here," Peacock murmured. "I know you're wearing that thing to fit in for our sakes more so than your own." He frowned. "Hopefully your efforts will keep me out of a certain harem."

Alex held up a palm when Vlad opened his mouth to apologize. Her crew had always respected her as a tough leader. She didn't want them responding to her like a girly-girl with soft feelings just because they now had a pretty accurate guess as to what she looked like naked.

"Hey, this isn't necessary. Really. You were shocked. I don't blame you. Let it go, okay?" She waited for their nods then turned the subject. "Keep very alert while we walk," she said under her breath, her gaze flicking toward Fija. "We still don't have a clue as to what all we're facing out there so I want you ready to rumble at a moment's notice."

"Got it," John said, nodding.

"My Laser-5 is fully charged," Vlad added. "I'm ready."

"Me too," Peacock sighed. "I can hardly wait to explore the great red yonder," he said sarcastically.

Alex snorted at that. "Just try not to be too feisty in front of the ladies, oh black-skinned one of the foul temper. I'm a bit too tired tonight to fight to the death over you." Her eyebrows rose. "Maybe tomorrow."

CHAPTER SEVEN

She kept alert, her eyes constantly scanning the horizon for activity, as the group made its way up the steep, rocky terrain. The obsidian metallic mountains grew silvery in appearance the further they climbed, visibility drastically plummeting as the red-tinted air grew thicker.

Alex's eyes narrowed thoughtfully as she considered the quandary of Fija. Aside from the discrepancy in their height and basic musculature, there didn't seem to be much difference between them. She found it a bit odd that a hundred million years of evolution hadn't managed to change the human race very significantly and found herself wondering if there was perhaps more to the Amazon and her males than met the eye.

Surely something had to be different, she thought. Something more than gaining a few inches in height and possessing more innate muscle mass. But if there were differences, Alex had yet to discover them.

There was something peculiar, though. Something Alex hadn't picked up on right away and still wasn't certain meant anything. It was nothing really, an almost absurd observation, but twice in the last hour Fija had come to a dead halt and started…listening. That's all. Just listening.

The listening in and of itself wasn't peculiar. What was odd was that she seemed to be able to pick up on inaudible sounds and vibrations that not only Alex and her crew were unaware of, but sounds and vibrations Fija's own males didn't seem to pick up on either.

Or at least that was what Alex was beginning to hypothesize. She couldn't figure out any other explanation for the sudden stops they'd made followed by the Amazon's intent listening. Then again, nothing out of the ordinary had resulted from any of it, so she supposed it was possible Fija wasn't hearing anything the rest of them weren't. Maybe she was just paranoid and stopping every so often to make sure no threats loomed in the vicinity. Whatever the case, Alex's hand was securely fastened around her Laser-5.

The group came to a standstill when Fija once again lifted her hand and motioned for silence. Alex shared a curious glance with Peacock, who stood to her right, then trained her gaze on the motionless alpha female.

What is she listening for? Alex wondered, intrigued. *What does she hear?*

Fija was so still she could have passed for a statue. Not a single muscle seemed to flex as she stood there staring off into the distance, her head cocked in such a way it was readily apparent she was listening for…something.

"Fija," Alex whispered, "what is — "

"*Shhh,*" the Amazon's males hissed in unison. One of the harem visibly gulped. "She needs must listen," he shakily murmured.

A chill raced down Alex's spine in reaction to the male's nervousness. She had no idea what it was Fija was listening for, but only an idiot couldn't figure out that whatever it was, it wasn't desirable.

"They rise early," Fija said softly, her eyes unblinking as she continued to listen. "They hunt already."

The tiny hairs at the nape of Alex's neck stirred as she, too, began to sense some invisible ripple in the environment. She didn't know if she was imagining things or not, but she felt as though she could register a faint buzzing, almost a hissing sound, in the farthest corridor of her conscious mind.

Her eyebrows drew together. She glanced toward John. If his impassive features could be believed, he hadn't picked up on any strange sensations. Nor had Peacock, she thought perplexedly, as her eyes met his. Nor Vlad…

Alex blinked rapidly, purposely warding off the strange fog that had momentarily enveloped her. She shook it off as best she could, the foreign awareness creepy to her.

"Alex?" John murmured, one dark eyebrow raised. "What's wrong?"

"Nothing." She took a deep breath and expelled it. "Nothing at all."

"I think they've gone," Fija murmured. "We are too far uphill for our scents to be tracked."

"What?" Peacock snapped. "What is gone?" When the Amazon didn't so much as glance up at him, his nostrils flared. "Listen, lady—"

"Fija," Alex interrupted before he verbally tore into her, not in the mood to see a fight break out. Truthfully, however, she felt just as exasperated as Peacock. These social rules of females only speaking to males they owned were dumb to the point of being problematic. "What just happened? What did you hear?"

The Amazon blinked. She glanced up, her dark gaze finding Alex's. "They are called *loma* in our tongue."

"Loma?"

Fija frowned as she shifted her weapons belt further to the left. "There is no translation, which is why the device in your brain cannot decode it. The closest word I can think of for you would be...hmm...snake-worm, I suppose."

"Snake-worm," John muttered. "Great."

"The loma," Fija continued as she directed with a flick of her wrist for the group to resume walking, "are a lower order of predator than the Xandi. Not so advanced as the predator peoples, but brutal killers nonetheless. Perhaps more so."

Alex's mind was reeling with questions as she briskly walked to catch up with the topless, nearly naked Amazon. "You never told me about the Xandi either. I'm lost here. And I'd like some answers."

Fija sighed as her knuckles tightened around the pole she carried. The crystal-based weapon was about three feet long, six inches in diameter, and possessed an extremely sharp and obviously lethal tip. The pole weighed at least thirty pounds, yet her guide was able to manipulate it and keep it at the ready for hours on end without so much as a complaint, or even lowering it once.

"You confuse me, little warrior," Fija said, shaking her head. "How anyone cannot know of the loma, let alone the Xandi..." She sighed again, seeming to recall Alex's earlier confession to her. "Snake-worms are just as they sound...vicious snake-like belly crawlers that live below ground."

Alex's eyes rounded as she listened with rapt interest.

"They are carnivorous, exceedingly large, and perpetually hungry, so the Takuri avoid them at all costs." Fija scanned the horizon as she continued her explanation. "It is fortunate for us they did not pick up on our scents for we've only two females here to protect so many males."

"I can protect my damn self," Alex heard Peacock mutter from behind them. She ignored him this time, just as Fija did every time, for she was in Commander Frazier mode and was, therefore, far more concerned with extracting needed information than salvaging Lt. Williams's male ego.

Oddly enough, however, Fija chose this particular opportunity to actually break the social rules and answer Peacock back for the first time. Coming to a sudden stop, she whirled around to face him. Her jaw clenched. "Are you human?" she snapped.

Peacock frowned. "What do you mean, am I—"

"Answer the question and no more. Are you human or are you not?"

Their dark gazes clashed. "Yes," he hissed, "I am human."

"Then you need a female's protection," she said acerbically. "You haven't our biological prowess."

Alex's forehead wrinkled. She could tell by the way her crew was muttering under their breaths to each other that they had taken Fija's statement as an unwarranted slight against males. But a niggling suspicion told Alex that Fija had meant what she'd said in the literal sense, and that females in this world were able to do—something—that males physiologically could not do...

But what?

She wanted to know—badly. Whatever it was, it went without saying that Alex wouldn't have this evolved biological capability either.

Alex almost put the question to Fija, but thought better of it. She would wait until they were alone later, when the males of the Amazon's clan weren't around.

Alex recalled Fija's earlier warning not to reveal her name or the story of where the *Methuselah* crew had come from to anyone, so she was fairly certain showing complete ignorance of life in one hundred million and seven A.D. wasn't too brilliant as moves go. The harem males were probably already suspicious from her previous comments and questions, including the more recent ones regarding the snake-worms and Xandi. And, she recalled, they had already heard her speak her full name. Hopefully they thought she was joking.

"We will be completely out of loma territory within another hour," Fija dispassionately informed Alex as she turned around and began trekking uphill again. "Only then can we lower our guards."

Alex nodded. She found her gaze continually straying toward the slightly muddy red ground, not wanting any surprises to take her unawares. Living in almost absolute ignorance of what it was she was facing made her heart beat a little too rapidly and perspiration break out between her metallic cup-clad breasts. "And the Xandi?" she murmured.

"The Xandi." Fija sighed. "There is no safe place from our natural-born enemy, little warrior. Best accept that and be prepared to battle on a moment's notice at all times."

"But who are they?" Alex whispered, not wanting Fija's men to overhear their conversation. "What are they?"

"Your guess is as good as mine."

Alex looked at her quizzically.

Fija shrugged. "Verily, every female of the clans that has been captured by them has disappeared as though she never existed. No skeletal remains found, no nothing. Almost as if the ground opened up and swallowed them whole."

"How do you protect against them then?"

"We live up high in the furthest-reaching catacombs, dwelling in fortresses carved out of the sides of the great black mountains. The Xandi tend to strike from the air, so our shields are very rarely lowered. Not even when we needs lower them to save the life of one of our own species."

"Interesting," Alex whispered.

And just a bit frightening. Fija was, after all, scared of little to nothing. That a breed of predators could be so strong as to keep an entire fortress filled with warrior women too intimidated to lower their shields spoke volumes.

"But sometimes," the Amazon said softly, "sometimes they find a way in. On those occasions not even a mighty fortress is enough to stop them."

Alex swallowed past the lump in her throat. If nothing else, Fija was a great storyteller. She'd make an excellent addition to any camping expedition that involved sitting around a roaring fire at night, roasting marshmallows, and telling ghost stories — a human tradition far older than even the *Methuselah*'s crew. "Has anyone ever tried to get the humans back after they are stolen? Surely anyone who has lost a son or daughter to them — "

"No sons."

Alex blinked. "I beg your pardon?"

Fija absently gripped the pole tighter, her biceps flexing. "They take only our women. Never the males of our protection."

Now that was weird. "Huh. I wonder why?"

"None can say."

And those who could were never heard from again.

Alex chewed on her lower lip as she considered that. "You said they are predators. Maybe they don't like the taste of male meat?" A dumb supposition, but quite frankly the only one that made a damn bit of sense.

Fija chuckled, a rare grin denting her mouth. "Perhaps, little warrior. Perhaps." She shook her head slightly and sighed, a serious expression arresting her features. "Even if we thought we were strong enough to attack them outright, none amongst us would know where to look for the remains of our fallen warriors." She shrugged. "The war between Xandi and Takuri has raged on for over twenty thousand years, yet all this time later the location of their stronghold is still unknown to us."

The stronghold. *Stronghold...*

The word sparked a memory in Alex, a memory of a certain Zutairan man's holographic image preparing the crew of the *Methuselah* for the worst.

Tongor. The demons' stronghold, the Zutairan man had said, was in Tongor — Akron.

But that had been millions of years ago, Alex reminded herself as she walked in silence next to Fija up the twisting mountainside. Certainly these Xandi weren't the same demons the Zutairan had spoken of. From an evolutionary standpoint it didn't seem possible. However, she mentally conceded, they could be the evolved offspring of that mutated race, and therefore it was quite possible they'd maintained the same stronghold as their forebears.

Alex kept her thoughts to herself as the group made its way deeper into Takuri territory. Somehow she'd have to delicately probe for more information concerning the Xandi. She sensed that Fija knew more than she let on.

She sensed, too, the importance of getting the Amazon to confide in her.

* * * * *

Throughout the rest of the trek, curiosity bordering on obsession gnawed at Alex. She wanted to hear more about these predator peoples, the Xandi. Loosely translated, the word Xandi meant *night-stalker*. They were nocturnal hunters, Fija had explained. They mostly, but not always, stalked their prey by the waning moon, when a human female's senses were at their least acute, striking most often while she slept.

This information was the last the alpha female had spoken of her enemy. It left Alex with a lot of questions and no answers. Namely what in the hell the waning moon had to do with a human female and her senses.

And how to best avoid getting picked off in your sleep by the enemy.

These thoughts and a team of others plagued Alex as the group made its way to an enclave Fija had called Zala Fortress. The village was cloistered into the side of a silver-black metallic mountaintop, the air so heavily red-tinted this high up that she had a hard time seeing through it. Fija seemed to be aware of her difficulty and, squinting her eyes as if trying to figure Alex out, decided not to ask. She shook her head again instead, sighing like a martyr— something she seemed to do a lot in the commander's presence.

Alex was disappointed that they'd arrived just as the sun was setting, because almost nothing of how the fortress looked was clear. She was able to make out a couple of vague snapshots of the overall region, but even that was hazy. One minute the red smoke cleared a bit and they were being greeted by twenty dour-looking female warriors standing guard inside the walkways that ran along the perimeter's high walls. The next time she blinked they were inside the capital seat of the Takuri, being steered down a confusing series of corridors and back entrances that led to only who knows where.

"I don't like this," Vlad muttered under his breath. "We know nothing of these people and yet we follow them as though they can be trusted."

Peacock frowned. "I don't see much choice, bro," he quietly rebutted. "Between the women warriors of Zala in here, fucked in the head though they may be, and the predator shit outside, I'll take my chances with the ladies any day of the week, thank you just the same."

"I agree," John whispered.

Alex snorted at that. "Or so Fija says. We don't even know that these predators exist. It could just be a smart ruse to get us to follow willingly."

"But you don't think so," Peacock carefully drawled. "Or we'd be out there instead of in here."

"True enough," Alex murmured. "Still, there is a reason why I forbade you to remove your hands from your Laser-5s."

She might like Fija, but trust was another issue entirely. Trust had to be earned. For all she knew, they could have just been lured inside the stronghold of the very demons the alpha female accused the Xandi of being. She doubted it, but Vlad was correct—they didn't know the Amazon and her males well enough to formulate opinions on their trustworthiness or lack thereof.

"This isn't the time for this," Alex told her crew. "We'll talk later. For now keep your eyes open and your mouths shut."

John nodded. "Will do," he murmured.

* * * * *

Fija's lair was, in a word, surprising. In juxtaposition from the austerity of her personality, the red earthen catacomb she called home was lavish, decadent, and surprisingly airy for being carved out of a part of the black mountainside.

The catacomb consisted of two levels. The lower level contained the kitchens, servant quarters, work chambers, and a huge atrium that opened up onto the balcony gardens for gatherings and festivities. The upper level housed Fija, her harem, and the other females of the dwelling. All chambers of the catacomb possessed tightly packed red soil floors, black metallic walls, and an abundance of vibrantly colored native flora.

The technology, Alex noted, was interesting. The enclave's existence was one of complete communion

---

with nature. Even the electrical source the Takuri used for lighting, heating, and baking was emitted by a curious bright red vegetable indigenous to Zala called *veepa*. Fija had explained to her enraptured audience that the vegetable could be eaten only upon its death, after it dimmed. While it was alive, the force of its heat was so extreme as to sizzle a person upon contact.

The Takuri did not possess advanced weaponry of any sort in so far as Alex could tell. Neither did they seem to place much importance in the types of conveniences people had enjoyed in her day, such as floor tiling and synthetic foods. But these people clearly knew their natural environment and how to live in unity with it. She supposed they had to have some sort of synthetic technology—the translation device now lodged in her and the crew's brains was proof of that—but the Takuri definitely favored the natural over the artificial.

The same held true for clothing—or lack thereof. Alex's wary green eyes took in the sight of many naked women as she made her way next to Fija up a twisting incline that led to the catacomb's higher level. The males of the dwelling, she noted, were given loincloths to wear, the same as the males of the Amazon's immediate entourage. Alex supposed the Takuri men were only permitted to be non-attired in the presence of the woman they belonged to.

"Who are all these people?" Alex asked, her voice kept low as she followed Fija. "Are all of these women females of your family?"

She shook her head. "No. I've yet to birth a daughter so I've no heir to speak of. These females train under me. When they come of age and skill, they will be warriors and make their own way in the world."

"I see." She hesitated a brief moment, her mind racked with a thousand questions. "You said you have never bore a daughter. Have you ever given birth to a son?"

The Amazon's jaw and shoulders seemed to simultaneously tense. "Yes."

The single word held more chill than warmth. Alex supposed she should have taken the hint and backed off the subject, but curiosity overwhelmed her. "What's his name? How old is he? Where is he —"

"Enough questions!" Fija bellowed, surprising her. She came to an immediate halt and whirled around to face the commander. Clearly this was one subject she didn't care to talk about. She had never seen Fija lose her composure. "His name is Sol, he has seen five years, and he lives below stairs with the other servants."

She glanced away, her gaze distant as her voice lowered to a murmur. "He was weaned from my bosom six months past. Once a boy is weaned he is forced into servitude until purchased by the female who will protect him. Such is the law under the Sacraments of Takuru."

"You allowed your son to be turned into a slave?" Peacock hissed, the contempt in his voice apparent.

Fija's eyes narrowed. Her nostrils were flaring, her stance one of challenge. "It is our way, male," she ground out. "Do not question me."

"You said there would be a feast tomorrow," Alex quickly interjected, trying to change the subject. "What story will we give these other warriors about my origins?"

The Amazon hesitated, clearly torn between answering Commander Frazier's question and letting Peacock's slight go. Alex was glad when Fija turned on her boot heel and continued walking. She shot Peacock a frown, letting him know now was not the time to point out the foolishness of their laws. First they needed a better grasp of the crew's new environment and surroundings. They needed to understand what it was they were dealing with. The loma, the Xandi—it was a lot to take in.

"I do not yet know," Fija finally replied, waving a hand toward the bedchamber where Alex and her men were to be ensconced. "I suppose we will both have our answer at the morrow's noontime repast, little warrior." She handed a skeleton key to Alex and nodded toward the door. "This eve is yours to do with what you will. Be below stairs when the village bells thrice ring, announcing the commencement of noontime." She looked at Alex pointedly. "And be prepared to abide by the customs of our people."

"Customs?"

"You can wear the body-plate of a warrior upon first entering the feasting chamber, but such is not acceptable when sitting down to break bread with other Takuri women."

Alex hesitated, her expression cautious. "What do you mean?"

"It would be viewed as a challenge against my house and the warriors within do you break bread dressed for battle."

She prayed this didn't mean what she highly suspected it did. "So what do I wear then?"

The Amazon's frown was solemn as she turned on her boot heel and walked away. "We dine naked," Fija said from over her shoulder. "Best prepare yourself."

Chapter Eight

"You are near. I sense you. I can almost taste you..."

Alex stilled, the sensual purr of his voice caressing her neck like soft puffs of cool evening breeze. *"Am I dreaming?"*

It didn't feel like a dream. It was different from the other times somehow. In her nightmares she felt only fear and hatred towards...*him*. In this moment, however, terror and desire were at war in her body.

Desire. It consumed her with a ferociousness she couldn't explain.

"...Or am I awake?" she murmured.

She heard a low chuckle, but could see nothing. All her senses but one—sight—were engaged. She could feel his large, callused hands on her breasts, kneading them, tugging at her nipples until she moaned. She could hear his breathing grow heavy from behind her. She could experience every sensation there was to be had except for vision. And she wanted—craved—to see him.

Yet another new facet to the nighttime hallucinations. This was the first time Alex could ever recall wanting to see him.

"Soon, my beautiful," he cryptically answered. His voice was thick with longing. *"Very soon…"*

Alex blinked several times in rapid succession. Snapping out of the dazed state that had consumed her, her eyes quickly darted around the bedchamber. She released a pent-up breath and sat up in the bed.

She was in Zala, safely tucked in for the evening with her remaining crew. John and Vlad were sound asleep. Peacock was still awake. Shirtless and wearing the customary loincloth of male Takuri, he stood just outside the room on a small balcony, gazing out into the abyss of reddish-black nighttime air.

Lt. Williams must have realized he was being watched. He blinked, then slowly turned his head until he was looking at Alex. His gaze raked over her, one eyebrow arching. "You okay, Al?"

Her cat-green eyes must have looked as wild and desperate as she felt. *Get it together, Commander. It was only a dream. It had to be a dream.*

"I'm okay." She cleared her throat, then qualified her assuredness a little bit. "Just never forget our promise to each other."

"Stay together?"

Alex nodded. "But I'm more interested in the part about how if any of us turns up missing, the others pack-hunt until a survivor or corpse is found."

Peacock stilled. "I don't forget promises. Especially not ones like that. May I ask why you're bringing this up now?"

"I don't know."

He frowned. She sighed.

"Peacock, look—I don't know what's happening!" Alex ran ten agitated fingers through her long, golden hair. "Probably nothing."

He looked as unconvinced as she felt. "But...?"

"I keep having these weird dreams about some...man." Her forehead wrinkled. "At least I think they're dreams." *And I think he's a man.*

Lt. Williams was quiet for a protracted moment, and then, "You *think* they are dreams? What the hell do you mean by that?"

Alex shook her head. "I don't know," she murmured. "They have to be dreams, but they are so vivid, so real."

"Lots of people have dreams that feel real, Al."

True. And that knowledge was the only barrier standing between downright panic and her current state of mere apprehension.

Alex blew out a breath. "You're right." She rolled her eyes and smiled. "I guess I'm just on edge because I'll be exploring Zala without you three tomorrow. And then there's that damn 'noon repast' with Fija et al. After that—"

"Whoa! Back up. You plan to go looking around without us? What happened to *your* promise?" He crossed his arms over his chest. "Remember…safety in numbers."

Her eyes narrowed. "I'm not breaking our promise," she said firmly. "We are safe inside Zala, at least until after that luncheon. Don't ask me how I know that—I just do! Anyway, I think it'll be easier for me to poke my nose around the village without you three in tow. Given the way of life here, there are probably places males aren't allowed to enter, and it doesn't help our objective for me to run into complications like that. I want to find out as much as I can about this place before that damn lunch tomorrow."

Peacock grunted. "Okay fine. I still think we should go with you, but I see your point so I'll let that part go for now. But the other part…why do you think we might not be safe *after* that lunch?"

She shrugged, genuinely unable to answer that. "God only knows what will happen after these other warrior women get a look at me. They could accept me as one of them or…"

"…make you a sacrifice to one of their gods," Peacock muttered, finishing her sentence for her.

"Right."

Their gazes locked and held. "Peacock," Alex intoned, "you are more than a second in command to me. Hell, you've been like family these past several years—the only family Robert, God rest his soul, and I had."

He nodded. "The feeling's mutual."

"I promise you I wouldn't even entertain the idea of looking around alone tomorrow unless I was one hundred and ten percent positive that nothing will happen to me or the three of you in the doing." She waved his concern away when he looked ready to retort. "What's got me worried is that lunch. And, more specifically, this whole Alexandria the Great business."

"The messiah you told us Fija spoke of?"

"Exactly. I want to make certain I don't say anything tomorrow that makes me look like a heretic. If I can find a library, or the Takuri equivalent thereof, then hopefully I can read up on their beloved Alexandria the Great...and on all the things *not* to say."

He frowned, but conceded the point with a drawn-out sigh.

"All of our livelihoods are at stake here," Alex said with gentle patience. In this moment, she wasn't Commander Frazier issuing an order. She was a woman who wanted her longtime friend and colleague to see the reasonableness and necessity of her plan. "Otherwise, I wouldn't bother poking around downtown Zala tomorrow morning without you guys."

Silence.

"All right," Peacock slowly drawled, "but since you're going through the trouble, I think you should read up—if possible—on more than their savior."

"What do you mean?"

"I mean, I can't live like this." He released a slow, measured breath. "I just can't, Al. There has to be someplace else we can go."

Her smile was sad and full of understanding. She knew Peacock would rather be dead than exist as little more than the equivalent of a slave. So would John and Vlad for that matter. They were men from a different era, a different world altogether. Men who had been important and influential once upon a time.

"I know," Alex murmured. "Don't worry. We'll leave here one day soon and begin again—with our *own* set of laws and moral codes. But before that can happen, you know I need to find out as much about our new environment as possible. If we leave here beforehand, it's just a matter of time before all of us become food to predators we didn't even know existed."

"Agreed. And that's why none of us have said anything about this little detour into hell."

They trusted her, their leader, to find their way out of Zala and steer them toward a new life. Alex would be damned if she'd let them down. "And I appreciate that trust."

Peacock glanced away, back toward the red-black sky. "I hope you find something tomorrow, something useful. I'm ready for the detour to end."

"Me too," she assured him. She sighed as she fell back onto the bed. "Me too."

CHAPTER NINE

The next morning, Alex walked down the main street of Zala, her thoughts fully trained on the task at hand. She needed to find out as much about the Takuri—and their enemies—as possible. She had left Fija's dwelling at the crack of dawn with that agenda in mind in order to do what it was she did best—explore alien terrain.

The fortress nestled high into the metallic mountains was small, compact and looked to be well populated. The sector's perimeters, which were heavily flanked by jutting pikes and female guards, secured an area of terrain that was jam-packed with trading stalls, temples fashioned from silver and obsidian metallic ores, and homes for those who couldn't afford the more secured catacomb dwellings.

The red-tinted sky contrasted greatly against the gleaming dark structures, lending a brooding mysteriousness to an already eerie landscape. It was a sight she wouldn't have been surprised to see on any planet but Earth.

The sound of voices snagged her attention, so Alex cocked her head to the right. A group of females, most likely teenagers, lazed around on the wide steps of a learning temple. They were sprawled out in a leisurely semicircle around an older woman who had to be their teacher. The females were all naked, indicative of the casualness and familiarity of the situation.

"Who should like to recite 'Scroll Three, Verse Seven' from the *Book of the Dead Prophets*? Go on. Raise your hands now."

"I know it, Milady! I know the answer!"

Alex watched and listened with interest as a teenage girl shot to her feet at the teacher's nod, her apple-sized breasts bobbing up and down as she stood. The girl looked more than eager to show her knowledge off to her fellow students. Alex noticed, of course, that no male students were in the learning temple. Fija had mentioned earlier this morning that it was against the Fifth Sacrament of Takuru for males to be formally educated.

"Behold the Mighty One," the girl began, her voice as clear and booming as her stance was proud, "for She is the Giver of Hope and the Voice of Freedom. Behold the Great One for She is the Deliverer of Justice and the Avenger of Tyranny. From the belly of the terrible xandor beast the gods did birth the Protector of the people. A mortal. A human. A warrior-queen."

"Excellent!" the teacher praised. "You shall do well on the morrow's quizzing session, Leaz. Now who should like to answer the next question?"

"I would! I would!"

The teacher nodded to a pretty dark-skinned girl who eagerly took to her feet. "Good then, Ma'qari. Here is the question I put to you. According to the Seventh Sacrament, what proof have we that the male of our species is biologically inferior to the female?"

Ma'qari smiled as her shoulders straightened, obviously pleased that she knew the answer without having to give it much thought. "That's easy, Milady. The answer, naturally, is because they do not bleed."

"Excellent, Ma'qari," the teacher praised. "Your mother should be proud."

Ma'qari inclined her head. "The bleeding cycle of the female is in time with the moon cycle which is in time with the very universe the gods created. The gods blessed the female with the ability to self-cleanse, a superior attribute that lower animals, namely the gentle-minded male, lack."

"Pitiful," another girl said on a snort. "And to think some of their breed lobby for equal rights under the Sacraments of Takuru. They should feel fortunate those superior to them wish to care for them at all. What they ask for is profanity to all that's holy! The gods have decreed us their betters and so it is."

Alex lifted an eyebrow, bemused by the conversation. Males, females—apparently it didn't matter who was in power. The ruling camp would always find a way to legitimize the belief in their superiority.

"It makes my skin crawl to think I must mate with such an animal one day," Leaz said, frowning. "Why the gods made us dependent upon their seed to produce more females is beyond my reasoning."

The teacher's eyebrows knit together thoughtfully. "The male is not an abhorrent like the predator peoples, Leaz, merely lesser. It is your duty to care for them, to protect them from that which they are too inferior to protect themselves."

"Like children," Ma'qari argued. "Your skin wouldn't crawl at the thought of offering protection to a child now would it?"

"I suppose not," Leaz admitted after a brief hesitation.

"And my mother says mating is rather fun," Ma'qari teased. She grinned when the other girls laughed. "I plan to find out just what purpose the gods had in mind for the male as soon as I'm declared a warrior and able to offer my protection to them."

"I can tell you their purpose right here and now," another girl quipped. "Their purpose is to be on their backs, cocks standing stiff, waiting to be mounted."

Alex smiled at the ensuing sound of female laughter, imagining—much to her amusement—the frowns that her crew would be making if they had overheard this conversation. She expected they'd feel as though they'd taken a tumble through the rabbit hole. And for all intents and purposes, they probably had.

Shaking her head, she continued walking down the main street of Zala. It didn't take long to surmise that the village was a throwback to the ancient Greece Aristotle would have called home. The only difference in the structure of the temples and shopping stalls was that the core material used for assembly was metallic in appearance rather than marble, and usually black or silver in color. Otherwise, Zala could have been, architecturally and culturally, the matriarchal version of the glory that once was Athens.

"I've something to show you, little warrior."

The unexpected sound of Fija's voice startled Alex. She whirled around and frowned up at the bigger woman. "I wouldn't do that again if I were you. My first instinct when taken by surprise is to kill first and ask questions later."

The Amazon snorted at that but otherwise ignored her statement. "Come with me. I know what it is you're looking for so I know you will wish to see what it is I want to show you."

"I've been asking you for answers since the moment we met. You've held your tongue. Now you want to talk?" Alex waved away the offer. "Thanks but no thanks. There's nothing you can show me that I can't find on my own before the noon meal."

"As Protector of the Temple, I've access to every sector and building within the perimeter of Zala.

Including the one of most interest to you. You, however, do not."

"I'll take my chances." She turned on her heel to walk away. "There isn't a structure in existence I can't break my way into."

"My but my, we are as short-tempered as we are short, period." Fija rested a hand on her shoulder before she could walk off. "My males surrounded me the whole of our journey. Conversation was impossible and you well know it."

Alex turned around to face her. "And after that?"

For the first time since Alex had met Fija, the Amazon looked truly angry with, not to mention insulted by, her. "I was tired," Fija said slowly but distinctly, over-enunciating each word. "Thirteen days on foot for me with little sleep. There was only one eve of trekking for you."

Alex sighed. In her frustration and impatience, she hadn't considered that. Hell, she didn't even know why it was Fija had journeyed from Zala to begin with. Given all the predators that lurked outside the stronghold, there had to have been a good reason.

"I'm sorry," Alex said. "I should have given you the benefit of the doubt. You gave it to me upon hearing my story so I should have returned the favor."

The respect glinting in her eyes showed that the Amazon was appeased by her words. "Come," Fija said again. "You have questions." Her dark eyebrows shot up. "And I have answers."

* * * * *

Fija gave Alex an admittedly interesting tour of the city's main focal points. An hour and several stops later, though, and Alex was beginning to wonder if they'd ever get to the place the Amazon had promised to take her to — the one that would answer her most fundamental questions.

"Patience, little warrior," Fija murmured as if reading her thoughts. "We are almost there."

Another fifteen minutes of uphill trekking and Alex found herself gawking up at Zala's apex — and one of the most beautiful structures she'd ever laid eyes on. Made of a sleek material that resembled red diamonds, the imposing temple before her was set apart from the others, not only by its finer composite and unique color scheme, but also by the formidable hugeness of it. Where most temples, be they for learning or marketplaces, were ten to fifteen pillars wide, this one contained at least fifty of the spiraling architectural pieces.

"What is this place?" Alex asked.

"The Temple of the Dead Prophets," Fija answered with a reverence that could not be mistaken. "Inside are your answers, little warrior."

She cocked her head and looked Alex up and down. "And hopefully mine, too."

Alex hesitated for a brief moment as she wondered at her statement, then followed the Amazon to the mouth of the structure. Guards surrounded it on all sides, flanking every possible entrance. At first she feared they would try to keep them out, but much to Alex's astonishment, the guards bowed to Fija without questioning their presence, then moved to the side so they could walk past them.

"You are important in Zala." Alex stated it as a fact, not a question.

"I am."

"Yet another surprise." She threw her an acerbic look. "I see we are full of them."

"From any other woman," Fija said matter-of-factly, not breaking her stride as they made their way up a long case of twisting stairs, "I would take your tone as an insult to my house and challenge you to mortal combat—a fight to the death."

"So why not me?"

"Because I don't cut off my nose to spite my face." The warrior was quiet for a moment before adding, "And because I am hoping you are who you think you are."

Throwing a long, straight black tress over her shoulder, Fija threw a hand toward the lower chamber as they continued ascending from it. "The corridor below leads to another temple where our people come to pray. Each Takuri village has a protector-goddess and ours is Aleeda. It is from the all-knowing, all-powerful Aleeda that our warriors seek strength and wisdom. Her temple is open at all hours, a safe haven for all. But up here...only those granted access by me are permitted within."

Having reached the top of the staircase, Alex turned to face the Amazon. "You have been kind to me and my men. You brought us to your home and kept us from harm's way. For that reason, I feel gratitude toward you. But that feeling is sinking, Fija. I respect and admire you, one warrior to another, but I've reached my boiling point."

Alex didn't know how to explain in words the irritation she was feeling inside. This little tour was interesting, but the Amazon's earlier words still stung. "You are hoping I am who I think I am. What does that mean?" She waved an agitated hand. "I've told you who I am! My name is Dr. Alexandria Frazier, commander and captain of the ill-fated *Methuselah*. That is who I am. That is all I've ever claimed to be. *You* say I claim to be the messiah of Tukuru! *I* have never said such a thing."

Silence ensued as narrowed green eyes locked with equally determined brown ones. The next few moments were quiet enough to hear a pin drop.

"Come," Fija said softly, breaking the silence. "In the chamber ahead. We will both have our questions answered."

Alex warily followed. Something about all the enigmatic statements the Amazon was throwing her way made her feel a bit uneasy, but she kept the pace.

Ten armed guards flanked the doors to the chamber in question. Fija waved them away. They bowed, then parted to give them entrance. Alex followed the warrior inside, the thud of doors closing behind her a reminder they were in this warm earthen chamber alone.

Commander Frazier stilled as she got her first good look at what was inside. Her eyes rounded. "This is a…"

"Hall of Herstory."

The main atrium of the museum was the entry point. It led to a long, wide corridor, which in turn led to who knows where. The red earthen walls were teeming with caged, untouchable items from antiquity. Pottery, jewelry—even munitions Alex recognized.

"A Laser-5," she said quietly, absently running a hand down the bar of a cage that contained a weapon she was all too familiar with.

"That is its name?" Fija murmured. She watched Alex with rapt interest. "Laser-5?"

Alex nodded as she walked on to the next display. "It has a lot of juice."

"Juice?"

"Killing power."

"We found a few in the black waters, but we could never figure out how to use them."

"That was the point. They only open and engage by a series of secret maneuverings." She sighed. "It was the perfect weapon in my day because it was armory that the enemy couldn't use against you if they managed to wrestle it from you in a struggle."

Alex smiled as she arrived at the next display — the fender from a 2010 sports car. Robert had loved collecting classic automobiles like the Migimoto on display. Restoring them had been his favorite pastime.

The next display was a kitchen gadget that had made fresh, warm bread in a second flat. Alex closed her eyes briefly, recalling that she and her dead husband had owned that very model once upon a time.

This was getting to be too much. The trip down memory lane was hurting far worse than she had expected it would.

"What happened?" Alex softly asked. She took a deep breath and batted her eyelids to keep the tears at bay as she grabbed the bars separating her from a refrige-a-stove. "What happened to my people, Fija?" She turned her head to look up at the taller woman. Try as she had to school her features, there was no mistaking the moisture at the corners of her eyes for anything but what it was. "Why are they gone?" she rasped.

Fija studied Alex's gaze with a gentleness Alex hadn't known her capable of. "We don't really know," she murmured. "Not details anyway."

"Generalizations then?"

Fija sighed as her gaze absently took in the refrige-a-stove. "No. Not even that. These relics you see washed up on the shores. From them we have tried to discern our past. But until you?" She shrugged. "We didn't even know when these people—your people—lived. You say one hundred million years ago, so perhaps it is so."

"There was a war that devastated the entire planet." Alex's nostrils flared with anger toward the country she'd once called home. Thanks to a certain Zutairan man, she had a pretty good guess as to what had befallen humanity as she had once known it. "What I meant was after," Alex clarified. "What came after the wars?"

Fija spoke as they resumed their walk down the corridor. "From what we can gather from the few relics we have found and been able to decipher, instant death for most. Of those that did survive the wars, famine and disease wiped out the majority of humans that were left. Very few made it through the decades following the aftermath."

"But some did."

"Yes. Some did."

Alex absently took in the sights as she was given her history lesson. "They were different from my people?" she asked. "Nobody could survive a biochemical and nuclear war without their body chemistry evolving to shield them."

Fija shook her head. "I do not know. You ask me to speculate on things my people hold no answers to. Over the course of what you are saying has been one hundred million years of evolution? Perhaps."

"And the changes to humans could be..."

Fija came to a halt and met Alex's rapt gaze. "In the beginning of time as the Takuri know it, the predators became stronger, faster, and more agile. Not to mention bigger...and smarter. The Takuri had to as well, to flourish and multiply. Or at least, such is what the *Book of the Dead Prophets* tells us. We have no other herstory to go by."

"So," Alex said, thinking back on the principles of Darwinian evolution, "those humans who were the fastest, the strongest, and who could cunningly elude predators, survived long enough to produce offspring. Those who didn't possess said attributes died off, and their inferior genes died with them."

"Something like that."

"But over the course of millions of years of evolution..." A frown marred Alex's features. "I don't know what I'm trying to say," she muttered, "but certainly more happened to the biological structure of humans than being strong, fast, and agile."

"Undoubtedly."

"Then…?"

"I do not know. I've nothing to compare us to. At least not until…you. *If,*" she emphasized, "you are who you say you are, little warrior." Fija shrugged. "Other than the *Book of the Dead Prophets,* Takuri possess no knowledge of years gone by — according to you, one hundred *million* years gone by."

"Do you think I am who I say I am?"

Silence.

"Yes," Fija said softly. "You look different, you carry an unfamiliar scent, and you are convincingly ignorant of our world." She sighed. "This is why I brought you here. To find out the truth."

Finally they were getting somewhere. "And you will do that how?"

"Follow me," the Amazon murmured. "Into the most sacred lair of this temple."

Goose bumps zinged up and down Alex's spine, but she followed nevertheless. She had no idea what it was Fija meant to show her, but gut instinct whispered it would finally — *finally* — answer her questions.

Her host led her down a literal maze of corridors, up three sets of twisting staircases, and then through another series of narrow halls. Finally, they reached their destination — the entryway to a chamber that was, again, flanked by female guards. Just like before, the women warriors bowed to Fija's authority and permitted them unquestioned entry.

The further up they got, the less ventilated, and therefore hotter, it became. For once Alex was grateful for the conical hat she wore. It kept her hair up and off her perspiring neck. Fija, all but naked, didn't seem to be affected by the heat.

"What about men—human males?" Alex asked as the doors behind them were closed and the Amazon prepared to open one final door. "Why are they lowly chattel in this world? Are they biologically inferior? What?"

"In some ways, yes, but in other ways, truth be told, no." She sank an antiquated looking skeleton key into the door they stood in front of. "But biology has nothing to do with the reasons behind shielding them from knowledge."

Alex quirked an eyebrow.

"Tradition needs be upheld because they are weak-minded," Fija said. "Under male dominion, your people died off because of male greed, pilfering, and perversion of nature." She turned the key in the lock. "The *Book of the Dead Prophets* proclaims it thusly."

"I see."

Alex couldn't offer an argument to that. Men had, in fact, caused every war Earth had endured in so far as she was aware. Or at least that was how things had been before the *Methuselah* left Earth. It was hard to say what the world was like during those crucial years Alex and her crew had been removed from it. Who knew what clout women had held during the years just prior to the biological and nuclear wars? Alex didn't. Fija didn't, either.

"What is the *Book of the Dead Prophets*?" Alex questioned as they entered the most sacred of the temple's chambers. "Is it housed in here? Can I see it..."

Her voice trailed off and her eyes widened. "Oh my God," she breathed out.

Alex's jaw went slack and her heartbeat raced as she came face-to-face with the statue of a woman who was a dead-ringer for someone she knew very well.

Herself.

"Behold the Mighty One," Fija whispered, inducing Alex to swallow roughly. "For She is the Giver of Hope and the Voice of Freedom. Behold the Great One for She is the Deliverer of Justice and the Avenger of Tyranny. From the belly of the terrible xandor beast the gods did birth the Protector of the people." Their gazes met and held. "A mortal," Fija murmured. "A human. A warrior-queen."

Alex's entire body was shaking. How? This couldn't be! It made no sense.

"Alexandria the Great is our savior as foretold by the prophets. She is to free us from hands far more wicked than that of any human male."

Alex said nothing. Just stood there as still as the statue of herself.

Fija's sharp gaze drank in her shocked expression. "Her name," the Amazon informed her, "is Dr. Alexandria Frazier, Commander of Methuselah. We always believed 'Methuselah' to be a city unbeknownst to the tribes."

"This is impossible," Alex breathed out, her eyes unblinking as she stared at the metallic thirty-foot statue. Shaking like a leaf, she felt this close to passing out. "This can't be me."

"You are a bit short," Fija quipped. Her smile slowly evaporated into a solemn frown. "But I saw you emerge from that xandor beast myself. And, what's more, I watched in awe and shock as you defeated it."

No — no, no no!

"Anyone carrying the kind of ammunition I had on me could have done the same," she protested, resisting that this woman of legend could be her. She was just Alex—plain old Alexandria Frazier! "That doesn't make me...*her.*"

Fija's spine went ramrod straight. "That is what we are here to find out."

The pronouncement gained Alex's wide-eyed attention. "How?"

She nodded towards the statue. "At her base lays one of the relics that washed up on shore from the black waters thousands of years ago. It is the hand impressions of the true Alexandria the Great. Many have claimed to be her, but none have matched up to her hands. They are, for a Takuri, rather...small."

Oh shit. "I see." Alex cleared her throat. "And what happened to the women who claimed to be this great messiah? I mean, after it was discovered they were liars?"

"They were declared heretics and offered to the xandor beast as a sacrifice to Aleeda. By sacrificing them to the same belly it was prophesized the true queen of our people would be birthed from, we knew that Aleeda would reward us."

This was just terrific. In so far as Alex could tell, one of two things would result from this morning's trek to the Temple of the Dead Prophets—she would either be branded a heretic and murdered, or she would be declared Alexandria the Great...the queen of a people she had no desire to lead.

She had promised Peacock they'd move on and take their morality and life ways with them. And that is exactly what she would do no matter what.

It would pain her something awful to take Fija's life, but nobody was killing her off. Her crew needed her. Patting her side to make sure her Laser-5 was ready to detonate, Alex made her way to the base of the statue—the statue that was a dead ringer for *her*. She still couldn't get past the striking similarities.

Similarities or not, she knew it couldn't be her. Alex was one of the best commanders NASA had ever known, but a queen she was not.

She stilled as she reached the base. Her eyes rounded in shock. The "hand impression" she was staring at was a three-dimensional DNA identifier

NASA required of all crewmembers. And that particular identifier, she realized on a rough swallow, was undoubtedly hers.

Oh. My. God.

"This can't be," Alex breathed out.

"Place your hand on the impression."

Alex blinked, snapping back to reality. She turned her head to look at the Amazon—a woman of unwaveringly grim appearance who had...*tears* in her eyes? "Fija?" she murmured.

"You are the one," Fija whispered. "I know you are." She batted back the tears. "I've been searching for you my entire life," she rasped, "oft trekking to the black waters in hopes of finding you."

Alex closed her eyes against the heartfelt words. She didn't want to disappoint Fija, but their dead prophets had been wrong. She was nobody's queen, let alone the sole hope of what was left of the human race.

"Place your hand on the impression," Fija reiterated. "I needs must know."

Alex's eyes flew open. Taking a deep, steadying breath, she placed her shaking right hand on the DNA identifier.

A perfect fit.

The automated voice Alex had known she would hear startled Fija who held her weapon up and prepared to battle. *"Good morning from NASA, Commander Alexandria Frazier."*

"It's okay," Alex said softly. "It's just a computer."

Fija's eyes were rounder than Alex's. "It knows your name."

"Yes. It was programmed to."

"What is a computer?"

"Hmmm…hard to explain. Synthetic technology. Much like your translation device."

The Amazon visibly relaxed. "I don't have a care for disembodied voices."

Alex would have smiled, but the next thing she knew, Fija had dropped to her knees before her. "You are the one," she announced with reverence, awe, and unmistakable hope. "I have found you. I scarce believe it, but I have fulfilled my destiny and found you."

CHAPTER TEN

Asleep for over a thousand years, air rushed into the lungs of Malik Ahmose. Fangs exploded from his gums. He hissed, serpentine-gold eyes flying open on an expelling of air. Nearby, a young female servant fell to her knees, her eyes closing from the power of the moment.

The king had awoken.

Flying up to her feet, she shakily ran from the sanctuary, screaming out the news to all within earshot. The shock and wonder evident on the buzzing crowd's faces as they followed her back into the sanctuary radiated the young girl's feelings precisely.

The prophecy had been fulfilled. He had arisen.

Perspiration soaked the king's hairline. He looked to be in pain, his face scrunched up as he shook and roared.

"She is near," Malik ground out. Slowly, he turned his head from where he lay in the coffin fashioned of pure gold. His intense gaze met that of the worshipful crowd, honing in on the warriors nearest to his position. "Bring her to me."

* * * * *

Alex walked from the temple with Fija in silence. The events of the last hour left her feeling confused, dazed, and uncertain as to what she should do or say. A queen! Her? The Takuri expected their prophesied "one" to free them from the Xandi—the predator peoples. How could a woman who'd never even seen a Xandi do for them what they had been unable to do for themselves?

What's worse, Fija planned to announce Alex as Alexandria the Great to her key warriors at the noon meal today. Word would spread throughout Zala by evening. And then Alex's life would change forever.

"Fija?"

"Yes, my queen?"

She sighed. The only good she could see coming of this was being able to wear her body plate to the noon meal. She figured a queen could do what she wanted. "Your *Book of the Dead Prophets*...who wrote it?"

"The three scrolls which comprise the sacred text were written by three different prophets. Two were Takuri seers, women gifted of the third eye, the second sight. The first scroll was written by an unknown prophet. Our people do not know from when he heralds. But it was he—a male prophet— who warned the Takuri of what befalls humans under male rule."

"What do you mean?"

She cleared her throat and recited a verse from the first scroll. "'Mankind is perverse in its plundering and greed. In the quest for knowledge and power, we have destroyed our own people.'"

Alex's teeth sank into her lower lip. "Mankind" had been a generic term in her day, one that referred to all people, male and female alike. She decided that now was not the time to point that out. "This prophet...you don't know from *when* he heralds, but do you know from *where* he heralds?"

Fija shrugged as she took long strides, more interested in getting to the noon meal and making her announcement than in explaining things she could talk about later. "He was born in a place called Zutair—"

Chills coursed down Alex's spine.

"—but none know where this Zutair was."

Alex's mouth went bone dry. She *did* know where it was. The area that once was Houston, Texas.

Of course! Suddenly things made sense. Alex didn't know the Zutairan man's name either, but *he* would have been one of the few to know about the possibility of the *Methuselah* reaching Earth intact...and that Dr. Alexandria Frazier was its captain and commander. He was probably the same person who had somehow managed to leave behind her NASA DNA identifier. The mission was top-secret. Very few knew about it. But he would have.

That explained one "prophet". He wasn't a prophet at all, just a scientist. But what of the other two, the seers? It was harder to explain those two away, scientifically speaking.

"Fija, we need to talk. I —"

A shrill scream pierced the air, inducing both women to whip around. And then there was another scream. And another. And another.

"What the…?"

"Come!" Fija ordered, grabbing Alex's hand. "The Xandi attack! We needs must hide you until we can strategize!"

But Alex was too busy gawking to hear her, let alone listen. She watched in horror as seven winged predators swooped down from the red-tinted skies and hunted.

"Oh my God," Alex murmured. "What are they?"

They were unlike any species she had ever before seen. The closest comparison she could come up with was a reptilian-like animal she's encountered in another galaxy. But that creature had been docile and friendly — these things were anything but.

At least ten-feet tall from head to talons, the winged invaders possessed the imposing musculature, sharp claws, and sleek bald heads of fabled gargoyles. Their black skin was tough and reptilian, their eyes a serpentine gold.

Alex stilled. *Serpentine gold…*

Her heartbeat raced. Perspiration broke out between her breasts. She'd know that gold gaze anywhere—it had haunted her enough in her dreams. One of the creatures might not be *him*, but they were definitely of his kind. Suddenly, the details that once were hazy became bone-chillingly clear...

He was a Xandi.

What the hell is going on?

"Come!" Fija implored her. "We needs must go!"

Alex blinked. She shook off the cobwebs that had enveloped her. Just as she was about to obey Fija and run, the sound of a girl's screams reached her ears. It was Leaz—one of the students at the learning temple. Naked, she was shrieking and wailing and begging for mercy as one of the brutish Xandi plucked her up from the ground.

No—no! She's just a young girl!

Her pulse racing, Alex snatched a poison-tipped knife from her boot and flung the weapon with deadly accuracy at her target. It struck him in the forehead. He released Leaz with a bellow before stumbling to the ground. The young girl shot up on two wobbly legs and scurried off as fast as she could.

The remaining six creatures seemed to still as they watched their comrade fall to the ground. Six sets of serpentine gold eyes turned to where the knife had been thrown from and honed in on Alex and Fija.

"Move!" Fija ordered. "Now!"

Alex needed no further prompting. Adrenaline surged through her as she realized the Xandi knew it was *her* that had thrown the poison-tipped knife. They studied her for a moment as though they'd never seen anything like her, then, simultaneously charged.

Shit.

Alex and Fija ran like mad, but Fija was faster, much faster. She moved with the agility and speed of a panther, reminiscent of the bionic woman. Apparently not aware that humans from Alex's day couldn't move like she did, it wasn't until Alex has been snatched up by two reptilian hands that Fija realized she was alone. Alex's screams gained her undivided attention.

"Noooooo!" Alex heard Fija cry out. "Ah gods— *noooooo!*"

PART III:
THE AWAKENED

CHAPTER ELEVEN

For a thousand years, he had slept. Just as the mage had predicted, a king had risen precisely one thousand years to the day of his first death.

Trapped in a state between the dream world and the conscious one, Malik had understood that he was the one. It wasn't until his mind had found *hers* that he knew the time of his evolution to be almost complete.

The link had been tentative at first, but grew clearer and stronger with every passing eve. She was courageous and brave—a warrior, a leader to her people. She would never succumb to him willingly. She was...

Everything he had known she would be.

Everything the seers had predicted her to be.

But she—this human woman—was so much more than that. She was also the key to ending the war that had raged on for twenty thousand years between the Takuri and the Xandi. She was the prophesized queen of all mortals, the one the mages had warned their race of.

Do I kill her outright or do I send her back to the Takuri after mesmerizing her?

It was the very question that generation after generation of clerics from the Ziggurat had spent their every hour debating for thousands of years. When the time came upon them that the prophesized king arose and Alexandria the Great became his prisoner, should the sovereign kill her...or claim her and bring her to his side? *Could* he bring her to his side?

To the frustration of the Xandi, the ancient seers never spoke of which king would rise again, let alone which of the two paths to take. As a consequence, all kings were housed in the sanctuary upon their deaths, while generation after generation of servants attended to them. They watched over them for a thousand years, incinerating their preserved remains and naming a new king only after they failed to wake up.

Malik had been different. Malik had awoken. But the question remained, what was he, the now immortal king of the Xandi, to do with the mortal queen of the humans?

Killing off this so-called Alexandria the Great seemed the most logical decision Malik could make. But what if, the clerics had long argued, what if her capture and death only made her a bigger martyr to her people? What if the Takuri—up until now too terrified of the Xandi to venture into their realm— took the offensive and declared all out war?

Fortunately for Malik, there was time to figure out what had been, until this morn, a hypothetical question. The stronghold of the Xandi was unknown to the human resistance. It would take them time to locate the heart of their realm, if indeed they ever dared cross the black waters to find it at all.

And so what if they did find it? Unless the humans had developed superior weaponry during his hibernation and evolution, it wasn't as though they could defeat the predators. Biologically, they were too inferior. The Takuri were sometimes able to stave off the Xandi with their villages' protective shields, but defeating the night-stalkers outright was an entirely different matter.

However, there was a lot to be said for numbers. The fact that the Takuri outnumbered the Xandi five to one could not be dismissed out of hand. The humans were like locusts in their ability to multiply.

Do I kill you, beautiful Alexandria, or do I bring you to my heel?

She was stunning in the dreamstate. He'd never gotten a good look at her face, just an overall impression of her scent and beauty.

He didn't want to kill her, that queen. He would do what he had to do, but in all truth he wasn't desirous of slaying her. Malik's jaw tightened as he ignored the servant girls bathing him and concentrated on the reality of the situation.

The process of evolution had been slow and hideously painful. He was an immortal now. Superior in his strength and more acute in his senses, but the price he had paid for being the chosen king of the gods had come at the cost of near insanity.

In his first life, Malik had endured more wars, battling, and bloodshed than even he could recall, but nothing could have prepared him for the mental anguish inherent in a thousand years of isolation. Being able to feel, but not to move. Being able to hear, think, and smell, but not to speak...

Madness had all but consumed him.

In the mercilessly long years spent between life and death, it had been *her* presence that had kept him sane — not another of his race, not one of the gods, but a human. In the beginning she had battled him, raged against all that he was and all that he would forever be.

Over time her stance toward him had changed.

Malik wondered, not for the first time since his awakening hours hence, how much, if any, of the communal dreamstate the human woman remembered. They had shared years together — hundreds of them.

Malik was no longer the same warrior he had been prior to hibernation. How could he be when madness had all but consumed him? Every hour made him more ferocious, every minute more merciless, every second a step closer to succumbing to the pain and torture the gods had forced him to endure. And then, just when he thought he could withstand no more, she, this human, had entered the dreamstate with him.

Alexandria the Great had redeemed him.

His nostrils flared. Redemption or no, King Malik Ahmose *had* to finish out the course the gods had set him on. It was his destiny to bring an end to the twenty-thousand-years-long war that had raged on between the Takuri and the Xandi. He had risen from the sarcophagus within the pyramid that had been erected to house him in his death. And now, once again, he ruled with an iron fist in the Ziggurat forevermore.

Will you rage against me in life as you did in the dreamstate?

Soon he would have his answers. The warriors were returning with her even as he bathed. He could sense her, could smell the familiar scent of her.

His cock grew stone hard with thoughts of fucking her. In the dreamstate, they had mated. He wondered what the reality of her tight, sticky flesh would feel like. Wondered, too, if he should touch her. Such could make disposing of her more difficult, if it came to that.

But can you stay away from her?

Malik was given no time to consider the answer to his question as the bathing servants immediately responded to his fierce erection. They moaned as they kissed all over his body and took turns licking and suckling his cock. His teeth gritted from the pleasure of it as he watched the three gorgeous, busty servants attend to his manhood. He had a thousand years worth of seed saved up and was more than eager to spurt it.

"My lord," a fourth servant interjected. She entered the underground bathing pond and, stopping before him, bowed.

Malik placed his arms behind his head and enjoyed the suckling. His heavy eyelids took in the sight of the naked servant, lifting slightly to reveal the slits of his golden eyes. "Yessss?" he hissed, his fangs visible.

"Your prisoner has arrived. She is caged and your warriors await your next order."

He stilled. So much for spilling his seed. That would have to wait.

Or maybe not.

Shooing the bathing servants away from him, he stood up and stared at his reflection in the mirror-silver waterfall whose waters whooshed down to fill the bathing pond that he stood in. While in this form, he decided, there wasn't much difference between a Xandi and a human male. Only the slits of his serpentine-gold eyes, his ever-present fangs, and his taller and more muscular stature hinted that he was not of their race.

On a growl, he shifted, taking on his impenetrable form. There were two faces to every Xandi—the animal and the man.

King Malik Ahmose, the prophesized immortal ruler of the Xandi, would meet his destiny as his stronger, invulnerable self.

CHAPTER TWELVE

Alex came to on a gasp. Startled by the intensity of the ice-cold water being sprayed at her, it took her a few seconds to realize she was naked. And, worse yet, naked in a cage.

It hadn't been a dream. The past several hours had been hauntingly real.

"Cease this!" a deep male voice bellowed. Alex's nipples stabbed out from the frigid chill. "Why did you not have her bathed for me in the fashion I commanded?"

"I tried, Almighty One," another male voice demurred as he turned off the jets of water. "Beg pardon, but she attacked me."

"Typical primitive human behavior." The first voice sighed like a martyr. "Depart. I needs must speak with the human queen."

"May the gods be on your side," the second man muttered. "Even one so great as you shall need their aid with that one."

Alex's head slowly came up just in time to see the retreating guard wave an agitated hand in her direction. They exchanged glares, as they had at least a dozen times over the course of the past several hours. Her jaw dropped open when, a second later, she watched the seven-foot tall, gold-eyed man with vampire fangs change—right before her eyes!—into one of those ten-foot tall, winged, black creatures.

Holy. Son. Of. God.

He smirked before lunging off two powerful thighs to take flight. She could only gawk in response, her eyes round and heart pounding.

This was new information. She'd seen quite a bit since her capture, but nothing could have prepared her for seeing...*that*.

When she had first been captured by the Xandi warriors, Alex had been assaulted by fear the likes of which she'd never before experienced. Being held prisoner by six beasts that resembled the genetic result of a union between black reptiles and winged gargoyles would have sent terror coursing down the spine of anyone. Not knowing what they meant to do with her, and assuming they would probably make a meal of her, had made the five-hour flight all the more harrowing.

They had toyed with her fear during the journey, thereby intensifying it, laughing and cackling as they shredded her clothing. Four of the beasts had held her suspended in such a fashion that, midair, she resembled a woman who'd been tied spread-eagle to a bed. Another Xandi had laughed as his immense body hovered over her much smaller one. He kneaded her naked breasts, plumping up her nipples by running reptilian fingers over them and pinching them until they were stiffer. Then he played with her vagina, remarking to the others that he'd never seen hair the color of which shielded her head and mons.

With every second that ticked by, Alex had grown more certain that she would be gang-raped—taken by force by a group of monsters. Especially since a sixth Xandi kept growling at her that he hoped the king let them fuck her as repayment for the death of the slain warrior he carried in his arms.

But then they had brought her here...wherever *here* was. After that they retreated.

"We are different from your kind."

Her head snapped up. She met the golden gaze of another creature, this one in his gargoyle-like, black, reptilian form. She stilled, a weird déjà vu knotting in her belly.

Their gazes locked. Alex's pulse skyrocketed. Her heart threatened to beat out of her chest.

Him. The one from her dreams.

No. Oh my G—no!

She didn't know how she recognized that he was the one, but she had never been more certain of anything in her life. In her dreams, she never really got a good look at him. And yet, she knew—*knew*—he was the one who had haunted her.

This can't be happening!

He was bigger than the other Xandi she'd seen. He stood at least half a foot taller while in this form. His musculature was even greater and more imposing, which was saying a lot. He looked like a behemoth ten-and-a-half-foot black reptile that stood upright and possessed wings. And those impenetrable gold eyes...

"Yes," she murmured, swallowing roughly, "you are different."

His forehead wrinkled in an arrogant manner. "*Ssss*uperior," he hissed. "Stronger. Mightier."

Alex's smile was anything but kind as her light green gaze raked over his features. "And uglier."

His smirk rivaled her own. "So say you now."

"So say I always."

He sighed, shaking his head. "You cannot defeat us, human. Ever."

An interesting turn in conversation. "I don't want to defeat you. I just want to be freed."

Silence.

"That is not a possibility. Ever. Our race does not release *any* human captives, let alone their prophesized queen. The question now is merely what do I do with you."

Prophesized queen? How could he know about that?

She was nobody's queen, damn it! She certainly wasn't prepared to die in the name of a people whose ways she didn't even respect. All she wanted to do was gather her crew together and leave this wretched place. It might take several years, but between Peacock, John, Vlad, and herself, she was certain they could put their heads together and assemble a working spacecraft. Maybe they'd return to Paleo. Lord knew that whatever hand evolution had dealt the Paleoliths, no race could have ended up worse than the ones down here on Earth.

Alex's jaw tightened. She came up on her knees to face him, her hands attempting to shield her nudity from him. "What you should do is let me go." She narrowed her eyes at him. "My men will come for me, you know. They will find you and they will kill you."

He laughed, a deep and powerfully irritating sound.

"Our weapons are superior," she said tauntingly. "Ask your dead warrior just how superior they are."

That reminder got him to quit laughing. "What was in that weapon?" he demanded. He was quiet for a moment as he glared daggers at her and then, *"Speak!"*

"Nothing you would understand." Alex concealed the inward wince she experienced from his show of anger. Her voice came down in timbre. "I have no desire to kill you, but if you don't release me my men will kill all of you without hesitation."

He wrapped his reptilian fingers around the bars of the cage, the talons from every finger jutting chillingly close to where she sat. The cage wasn't large at all—maybe just long enough to fit one of his own race inside of it. Having menacing pikes loom so closely served as a deadly reminder of its small size.

"You keep saying your *men*. Do you think me a fool, little one? Takuri do not permit their males education, let alone weapons," he hissed. His expression was one of superior knowing. "We have studied your kind and brought them to heel for thousands of years. We know your ways, human."

"I am not one of them."

"Cease shielding your body—*my* body—from me. Lie down on your back and spread your legs."

Alex blinked, momentarily thwarted by the change in topic. And then, his words sinking in, her heart rate soared. "Never," she rasped.

"Now," he growled. "You are mine and I wish to see what you have to offer me."

She was frightened, but the chill in her voice was unmistakable. "I'd rather die."

"So say all Takuri...at first."

"And I repeat again, I am not one of them."

His gold-slit gaze wandered up and down the nude body she was trying so desperately to shield from him until it landed on her face. "There are but two races, little girl, Xandi and Takuri. Your *sssscent* is a foreign one and your coloring exotic, but this much I do know—Xandi you are not."

"Nor am I Takuri," she protested. "You wouldn't believe what I am." She sighed, a little bit of fight going out of her. "I don't even know what I am anymore."

Silence.

"You speak in riddles," he murmured. "And I don't have a care for it." His gaze locked with hers. "I will deal with you later, human. For now I order you to sleep."

He made to walk away, pausing long enough to threaten her. "Unless you enjoy your current 'home' and its nonexistent amenities, I suggest that you be more obliging toward me the next time I pay you a visit."

Her eyebrows slowly formed an inquisitive arch.

"When I enter this chamber on the morrow, spread your legs, play with your lovely pussy, and beg your king-god to fuck you."

Alex's heart began thumping madly. "Never," she vowed again.

His eyes glittered in mocking amusement. "So say you now."

* * * * *

Malik sat in silence in his formal dining chamber, uncertain as to what course he should take. He slowly sipped from the chalice of xandor blood and considered what had just transpired in the dungeon.

He had never—*never*—met an unmesmerizable Takuri female before. He hadn't even known such a thing existed. But this one? She had told him she was no Takuri. He wasn't about to admit it to her, but she had nigh unto convinced him upon their first meeting.

So much for mesmerizing her, then sending her back out amongst her people.

At least three times Malik had tried to mentally summon Alexandria into doing his bidding, but she hadn't responded to any of the attempts. And, as he had previously admitted to the mortal queen, she did in fact carry a unique scent. Then there was the issue of her hair and eyes...

By the gods that had awoken him, Malik had never seen hair and eyes the color of those. The hues were as foreign and exotic as they were beautiful. Her hair was a truer gold than the gaze of full-blooded Xandi, her eyes unlike any color he could name.

The dreamstate had taught Malik many things about Alexandria the Great, but it hadn't so much as alluded to the things he'd learned this day. Unmesmerizable? Had he not witnessed the phenomenon himself he never would have believed it.

Emptying the chalice, he swallowed down the remainder of the xandor blood. During his first reign, his mortal reign, xandor blood had always been able to give him a rush unlike any other type of elixir. At least one thing hadn't changed, he thought with a frown.

"Bring me another chalice," he ordered a nearby servant without glancing up. "Now."

"Perhaps you should kill her and be done with it, my lord," Ghazi said softly. The most trusted of his warriors, the gods had put Ghazi to sleep when Malik had died his first death. He had awoken not long after Malik. "If she cannot be mesmerized then—"

"She claims that her 'men' will come find her." His head came up slowly. Now in his man form, he was able to raise his eyebrows bemusedly. "And kill us."

Ghazi snorted at that. "Lies. We both know that."

"Do we?" Malik's smile evaporated. "She killed that Xandi warrior. And, what's more, she bespoke of the possibility of more such weapons."

Ghazi stilled. "Do you believe her?"

"I do not know." Malik stood up. Snatching the proffered chalice from the servant's grasp without so much as looking at her, he quickly drank down the xandor blood and handed back the ornamental cup. "But I do know I can't kill her until I exact more information from her."

"My lord?" Ghazi stood up, his eyes searching the king's grim face.

"I never wanted this so-called honor," Malik rasped. "Eternal life? Watching all those we come to know grow old and die? The gods can keep their immortality."

Ghazi's eyes widened. "You don't mean that bit of blasphemy…"

"Yes. Yes, I do." Wearing nothing but the traditional thigh-high leather skirt and boots of

Tongor, it was easy to see his muscles tense. "This war has raged on for tens of thousands of years—longer than that if the ancient scrolls can be believed. And now we're to accept as true that all Takuri will compliantly lay at our heels simply because we have captured their queen?"

"The mages said—"

"The mages said nothing!" Malik bellowed, teeth gritting. "The clerics read into their words that which they wish to see. Nowhere is it written that by killing or keeping Alexandria the Great that our race shall prevail."

"Surely you do not believe that their kind shall win the war?"

He shook his head. "I will not let that happen."

"Then?"

Malik frowned as he prepared to walk away. "I needs must figure out how much of the human queen's words are truth and how much is naught but bluster. And in order to do that..."

"She needs be brought to heel."

Malik walked off. From over his shoulder he growled, "She needs be brought to *my* heel."

* * * * *

Alex spent the remainder of the night feeling this close to losing her threadbare grasp on sanity. She had dreamt of this cage, this dungeon, and of *him*, for months. Now she was here—captured, naked, and enslaved.

It was no dream.

Drawing her knees up, she clasped her arms around them and slowly rocked back and forth. Long, golden curls, usually confined in a bun at the nape of her neck, flowed to mid-back, tangled and disheveled. Her green eyes were wild, her heart rate much higher than it should have been.

Alex believed in science and logical reasoning. A longtime avowed atheist, she had only given credence to the tangible and explainable. But how could she reasonably explain away what she had experienced all those months? Dreams were nonsensical flights of fantasy...

Weren't they?

She chewed on her bottom lip. Once upon a time, Dr. Frazier had scoffed and rolled her eyes at those people who claimed to have extrasensory perception—ESP. Now she was left wondering if *she* had been the true idiot. How easy it was to feel superior in her knowledge when she'd never encountered the same sorts of situations the "weirdos" had.

Alex closed her eyes on a sigh. Still rocking back and forth like a child who needed cradling through a storm, she spoke words she hadn't spoken aloud since she'd been a small girl forced to endure the boredom known as mass:

"Hail Mary, full of grace," she whispered, "the Lord is with thee. Blessed art thou among women, and blessed is the fruit of thy womb, Jesus. Holy Mary, Mother of God, pray for us sinners now and at the hour of our death."

Alex's eyes slowly opened. Shivering, she looked to the heavens and crossed herself. "Amen," she murmured.

CHAPTER THIRTEEN

Taking flight on a roar, King Malik Ahmose shape-shifted midair and flew at top speed down to the dungeon. If the dreamstate had taught him anything, it was that she wouldn't give in yet—not yet. Nevertheless, he understood that she would not break until he, himself, cracked her.

When he arrived at the cage, he found her asleep. It looked as though she'd endured an uncomfortable eve. A few more nights like that, with no food or water to make it even semi-bearable, and she would give in. Begrudgingly so, but it would come to pass.

"Let me guess," Alexandria said, surprising him with the knowledge she had awoken. Her voice was scratchy, her throat parched. "You want to kill me. Excuse me," she said acidly, her head slowly rising until two narrowed green eyes looked at him from beneath a sheath of tangled, golden hair, "you want to fuck me and then kill me."

The mention of fucking her gave Malik an instant, painfully swollen erection. He remembered their matings in the dreamstate even if she didn't. And there was no getting around the reality that he hadn't spurted in a thousand years. He should have given his cum to the bathing servants last eve, but thoughts of stroking in and out of the human queen, glutting himself on her flesh, had seduced him instead.

Kill her? He didn't know. Fuck her? Yes.

"*Ssss*omething like that," he said softly, unmistakable menace in his tone.

"I'd just as soon get it over with then." Coming up on her knees and throwing her hair over her shoulder, Alexandria bared her plump breasts and golden-haired mons to his view.

Her breasts were large, well-rounded, and possessed of stiff pink nipples. Malik had never seen pink nipples before. He couldn't help but grow more aroused upon seeing them, the gold slits of his eyes narrowing impossibly further in lust. And the patch of golden hair between her legs...

He frowned when it occurred to him she was getting the upper hand. Apparently the human queen recalled at least parts of their shared dreamstate. "You have not followed orders, slave."

She stilled. When her nostrils flared, Malik knew it was paining her to give in. Alexandria would just as soon die before being physically vanquished — that much he could easily sense about her. And yet she yielded, making him wonder why she was complying without a fight.

She was up to something. He needed to determine what that something was.

"Excuse me, let me try again," the human queen intoned.

Lying back on her elbows, she spread her thighs open as wide as they could go. Malik's pulse raced as he got a close-up view of her gorgeous, tight, pink cunt. He had never seen a woman like her and he knew he'd be lying to himself if he didn't concede that he wanted inside of her more than he wanted to breathe.

Alexandria began playing with herself, doing all those naughty things for his viewing pleasure that he had instructed her to do for him at their last meeting. She used one hand to play with a nipple—pinching and pulling at it until it was ripe and aroused. She used her other hand to play with her gorgeous pussy, running her fingers down its creases and folds until they grew slick and her breathing heavy.

"Suck on your nipple for your king-god," Malik murmured, his cock so hard it dripped pre-cum.

She immediately obeyed, one hand pushing up a heavy breast and her teeth latching onto her stiff nipple. She suctioned it into the warmth of her mouth and suckled it hard. Her other hand continued playing with her exposed cunt, teasing her tiny clit and rubbing it in brisk circles.

"Now," he said thickly, "release your nipple—*my* nipple—and beg me to fuck my slave."

"Please," she gasped, releasing her nipple from her mouth on a wet popping sound, "please fuck me." Alexandria played with her pussy faster, the circular motions at her clit growing harder and more intense. "I beg my king-god to fuck his slave's pussy."

"Cum," he ordered her, nigh close to spurting just from watching her. "Cum for your king-god."

Alexandria's nipples poked out impossibly stiffer as she moaned and played with her drenched cunt. She never met his gaze, but closed her eyes and followed his instructions instead. She rubbed her clit harder, a small groan issuing from the depths of her throat.

On a gasp, she came. Her eyes rolling back and closing, her nipples stabbed straight out. Her breasts rose and fell in time with her labored breathing, making the scene all the more seductive to him.

Malik's eyes took on a drugged look as he watched the human queen come for him. He wanted to fuck her—*needed* to fuck her. And he would.

In time.

"Very obedient," he purred, gaining her attention. "Your king-god likes an obedient slave."

Her nostrils flared just a bit before she schooled her features. Going back to her knees, she sat before him. This time she didn't bother trying to shield her breasts from his view. "May I leave this cage then?"

Silence.

"On the morrow," he murmured, "you will look me in the eyes while you pleasure yourself for me."

Her gaze widened, the desperation she felt a tangible thing.

Good.

"May I have some food?" she breathed out. "Water?"

"No."

Her head snapped up. At last she made eye contact.

"You are my *ssss*lave," Malik hissed, "My property, my possession...my personal fuck toy." His smile was filled with mocking amusement. "When I am further convinced of your compliance, I will consider giving you nourishment."

Alexandria's pretense at obedience immediately ceased. Just as Malik had suspected it would.

"Why don't you just kill me?" she snapped. Her teeth ground together as she wrapped her hands around the bars of the cage. "I'd rather die than be any man's slave, let alone a whore of the devil!"

Malik stilled. His serpentine gold eyes narrowed at her. "Perhaps a couple more eves down here will change your mind," he said softly. Too softly. "You needs must remember what you are, Alexandria, and then I shall consider letting you out of the cage."

Their gazes met and locked in challenge.

"What am I?" she gritted out.

"A fuck toy to King Malik Ahmose," he murmured. His expression was arrogant, but otherwise unreadable. "*My* fuck toy."

CHAPTER FOURTEEN

The coast was clear. Peacock motioned for John and Vlad to follow behind him, then led them to a hidden alcove where they could listen in on the meeting transpiring below.

Alex had been gone for two days now. He had no idea where she was, or if she was even alive, but was determined to get some answers. When Peacock had approached Fija yesterday, she had waved him off, insisting she had no time to deal with a male. "I needs must plan!" she had barked. It had been the last the crew had seen of her.

Until now.

"There she is," John whispered, inclining his head to the far right of the atrium below.

"Uh huh," Peacock murmured. "If we don't get answers listening in on this meeting, then we'll have to resort to drastic measures."

Vlad patted his Laser-5. "I am ready."

All three scientists watched with rapt interest as Fija took to the stage. Women warriors, all of them dressed in their *takus*—body-plates, bowed as she passed by them, then applauded as she ascended to the podium.

Peacock frowned. He decided it was too bad that the Amazon was the 100,000,007 A.D. version of a sexist Arab sultan. The woman was pretty. Damn pretty.

Fija began to speak. It was difficult to hear what was being said from so far up, so the men leaned in closer. Whatever the conversation, it was causing a great deal of fervor below.

"Are you certain she is the one?" one woman asked.

"I am," Fija answered. Her back went ramrod straight. "She passed the test. She *is* Alexandria the Great."

Shouts and cries punctured the air. Fija spoke again, but this time her words were inaudible to the crewmembers listening in from above. The female warriors of the assembly sounded to be troubled by whatever great announcement their leader had just made.

Peacock looked quizzically at the other two crew members. "They think Al's that woman foretold by their prophets?"

"I don't know," John said in hushed tones. "Sure sounds like it, though."

"Ssshhh," Vlad interjected. "Fija is speaking again."

The Amazon's stance was one of authority, her voice booming. "We needs must cross the black waters and find her! Our queen has been stolen by the Xandi and it is up to us, fine warriors, to save her. Without her...we perish. Such has been foretold by the *Book of the Dead Prophets* and so it is."

Peacock closed his eyes against the damning words. His commander, and more importantly his friend, was gone. His worst nightmare had been realized—Alex had been captured. His stomach muscles bunched.

Somehow Commander Frazier had known this was going to happen. He should have listened to his gut instinct two mornings ago and accompanied her into downtown Zala whether she'd wanted his company or not. But it was too late for "if only". Now, along with the other crewmembers, he had to concentrate on finding and rescuing her.

"We know not where the demons' stronghold lies!" a dismayed voice cried out.

"It matters not. We *must* find Tongor!" Fija countered, causing Peacock's eyebrow to hitch. "We can sit here and allow our queen to be murdered at the hands of our mortal enemies or we can take to the black waters and try to find her. As Protector of the Temple, I cannot sit idly by and hope for the best!"

Peacock had heard enough. Motioning to the other two men, they quickly and quietly made their way back to the bedchamber they'd been given to share with Alex. He turned to Vlad and John. "Tongor. You heard her say it yourselves."

John nodded. He ran a hand over his five o'clock shadow. "That's Akron, Ohio."

"It *was* Akron, Ohio," Vlad reasonably pointed out. "We don't know where that region is now any more than those female warriors do."

It didn't matter. Not to Peacock. And he knew the other men well enough to realize that it didn't really matter to them either. A promise was a promise and they would be keeping theirs—they would search for Alex until she, or—God forbid—her corpse, was found.

"You all ready to leave the rabbit hole?" Peacock murmured.

The men stood in silence, staring at each other for a suspended moment.

"I think," Vlad murmured, "the most logical assumption we can make is that the sun still rises in the east and sets in the west."

Peacock slowly nodded. "We'll use that as our compass then."

"I packed and secured our munitions last night." John took one last brief glance around the bedchamber before inclining his head. "Let's do it, bros."

* * * * *

Alex stared at nothing, her eyes unblinking, as she lay curled up in a ball in the back of the cage. She had thought that maybe, just maybe, she could get herself out of this cell quicker if she pretended to be obedient. She *had* to get out of the dungeon. There was no hope of escaping the Xandi otherwise.

Please find me, Peacock. Where are you? John? Vlad? Don't leave me here!

Her teeth began to chatter. Her mind felt close to splintering.

The beast—Malik—had said he would return "on the morrow". He hadn't. Alex had been given no chance to try and convince him, again, that he had broken her to the point of obedience.

Will you come tomorrow?

She was tired, cold, hungry, and oh so thirsty. Her throat was dry and parched. Hunger pangs kept her bowed over, their intensity sharp. Eventually, she knew, they would subside and she would feel nothing.

Then death would come.

The night became morning, the morning afternoon, and another day ticked by at a snail's pace. Alex realized that she could very well die in this cage; she realized it, but no longer cared. He—it—might never come back. This king of demons had merely toyed with her, giving her hope of living where none existed. So be it. If he meant to starve her, she prayed the end result came mercifully soon.

Every second felt like an hour, every minute like a day. For the first time in what she had once hoped to be a long life, Dr. Alexandria Frazier, commander and captain of the *Methuselah*, prayed for death.

"Let it end," she whispered, her throat so gravelly she could barely speak. Her lips were dry and parched. "Please just let me die."

* * * * *

She shivered from where she lay curled up in a ball on the red earthen floor, her arms wrapped around her up drawn knees, her eyes unblinking. She was cold, hungry, and broken — at last broken.

Just as he had planned. Just as he had always wanted.

He kept her in a cage, naked and half-starving, like a neglected animal in a zoo. Every day her will to resist him grew weaker and weaker. Every day the hunger gnawed at her belly until the pangs felt like sharp talons clawing at her gut.

She was weak. So fucking weak. She needed nourishment — food and water. Oh God, how she fantasized about water trickling down her dry, parched throat...

She would never be given water unless she did what he wanted.

No, she thought in horror. *How can I let that...that...thing touch me? How can I —*

"I would have your answer," he purred.

She closed her eyes against the sound of his voice. She was so frail that not even her hearing worked as acutely as it once did, for she hadn't realized until he'd spoken that he'd approached the cage. She could feel his devil's-eyes on her, though, just like always. Coiled up in a ball with her back to him, she still knew the precise moment when his eerie golden gaze flicked to her buttocks...and then onward to the folds of flesh visible between her legs.

That flesh was what he wanted. That and a whole lot more. He wanted things from her that were so sick and frightening they didn't bear dwelling on.

"Answer me," he hissed, "or I leave you here for another night."

By the morning she would be dead. And escape would be a moot point. Her body was so damn weak...

"Yes," she whispered. She closed her eyes tighter, feeling ill. "I've just consented to being the devil's whore."

His depraved laughter echoed throughout the underground cavern, reverberated against the impenetrable bars of the cage. "Much lower than a whore," he murmured. "At least a whore is permitted to live through it."

She wanted to vomit, could feel bile churning in her belly.

"Look at me!" he shouted, his voice angry. "You will look at me!"

Oh no—oh please no.

She drew her knees up impossibly closer against her breasts. She didn't want to look at him. Anything but that. Sweet God above, anything but—

"Look at me!" he bellowed.

And then he was in the cage, his hideous claws jerking her up from the ground, forcing her to her feet. She wanted to fight him, but she could barely speak or stand, let alone rage against him.

"Look at me!" he demanded, shaking her. "Open your eyes!"

No! No! No! Oh God, please don't make me look at him!

She'd never been more frightened. Her heart was thumping like a rock against her chest, her breathing sporadic and growing more labored by the second. She was afraid to know what he looked like for she'd seen his kind before. Hideous. Freakish.

Monsters.

"I said look at me!"

Startled awake by the loudness of the bellow, it took Alex a moment to realize that the last sentence had really been spoken. She hadn't dreamt it. Not that part.

Her eyes flew open. Her gaze met and clashed with a serpentine gold one.

In the dream, she had feared looking at him. In reality, his dramatic reptilian appearance no longer registered as significant. She was too weak, too close to death, to care. Some things about the dream, however, remained unchanged...

Alex was broken. She had never thought to be so desperate for life as to beg the enemy for mercy. Then again, she had never been so hauntingly close to death before. Genetic imprinting took over and the need to survive overrode all other thoughts and emotions.

Her head was too weak to lift it from the red earthen floor. She moved a shaky hand as close to the beast as she could. Her dry, cracked lips worked up and down, but it took forever to get out the two words she so desperately wanted to say. "Help me."

A large, deadly, reptile's hand enveloped her trembling one. Alex closed her eyes and fell asleep, uncertain if she would ever wake up again.

CHAPTER FIFTEEN

"Are you in need of aid, Your Greatness?"

Malik waved away the servant that had entered the bathing pond. He could and would attend to Alexandria the Great himself. Already he had fed her, though she hadn't been awake to know it. She would live.

In his man form, Malik looked down into her unconscious face. Guilt was an emotion he hadn't much experience with, and yet he found himself consumed by it now.

It had never so much as occurred to him that Alexandria would be nigh unto dead from a mere four days without nourishment. Takuri could last for weeks. Malik had thought four days without food and drink would make her more compliant, but kill her? He'd never heard tell of such a fragile creature as this one.

What are you, little one? You are an enigma to me and my race.

He ran his hand through her golden curls, as mesmerized by them as he was by her. Alexandria the Great, the prophesized queen of humans, was an anomaly. A contradiction of bodily frailty and superhuman mental strength. Her mind was superior to Takuri, and he begrudgingly admitted, perhaps even to the Xandi. And yet her body was a delicate vessel, small in its stature and quick to deplete the nutrients which kept it going.

She had told him she was no Takuri. What had once seemed impossible was quickly becoming more and more probable.

What manner of creature are you?

Malik bathed her naked body, running a large hand over her breasts. In the coolness of the bathing pond, her pink nipples stiffened and turned a riper, redder color. He bent his head and drew one into the warmth of his mouth.

Suckling from her nipple, his erection was fast and furious. He wanted her so badly that his entire body ached with need.

Now was not the time. But soon. Very soon.

Taking one last hard suck, he released her nipple with a popping sound. She moaned slightly, but otherwise didn't awaken. That was just as well. It gave him more time to think.

Malik gently bathed her, washing her hair, her body, her everything. His mind, immortal though it now was, couldn't fathom what this female was. The gods had prepared him for many eventualities in the dreamstate, but for the possibility that the queen of humans was no human? He didn't know what to make of this.

The war between Takuri and Xandi had raged on for millennia. It was so old that none knew why it had even begun, only why it continued—

His race needed human wombs.

Only captured humans—Takuri they were certain couldn't escape—knew this. To those who still lived as freewomen in the matriarchal societies high in the mountaintops, the reason for human females being hunted down was shrouded in mystery. It had to be that way. If they knew the reason why they were captured and mesmerized by the Xandi, it could very well give them the upper hand in the war.

Two cultures, two races, two opposing ways of life. The Xandi were ruled by males, the Takuri by females. The Xandi coveted the humans, but the Takuri loathed the Xandi. Such was how it had always been.

In the early stages of the war, when the Xandi had first discovered that human females could mother their offspring, their males had taken to the skies and attempted to steal as many Takuri as possible. It wasn't until a few generations later that they realized not all Takuri could be impregnated of Xandi seed—only certain females could. It took them another several hundred years to figure out exactly which human females they needed.

Those whom males of their race could enter the dreamstate with.

Naked, Malik carried Alexandria the Great's nude body from the bathing pond and up to a favorite smooth boulder where the red-tinted sunlight would dry her off naturally. The sound of the waterfall whooshing beside them was comforting in its familiarity. The people Malik had loved in his mortal life—his sire, his human mother, his brothers—all were long dead. But this glorious waterfall had not changed in a thousand years. It had been his favored retreat from the pressures of ruling Tongor a millennium hence, and so it was now.

Lying the human queen flat on her back, Malik came up on an elbow and stretched out beside her. He stared down at her through the gold gaze of his race, a large, strong hand running over the contours of her limp body. He plucked at her gorgeous, stiff nipples, went lower and gently rubbed her belly, then lower still until his fingers were sifting through the soft golden hair at her pussy.

He felt a connection with this woman, human or no. He had raged against it, told himself to be firm and unwavering, but in the end he couldn't deny it—killing her wasn't an option.

He had paced the ziggurat for days, angry with himself for feeling this weakness. What path was left to him was foggy, but that she could not die was as clear as the mirror-silver liquid of the waterfall. Malik could only be glad he figured these things out *before* she had expired from lack of nourishment rather than after.

He had shared the dreamstate with her. Whether this was indicative of the fact that she was the one — *the only one* who could sire his offspring — or indicative of the fact that they had experienced the mutual connection together solely because the gods had meant to prepare him for all that the prophesized queen was...

He didn't know. Verily, Malik didn't even know if an immortal could produce offspring. He was the first of any race to be gifted — or perhaps cursed — with this state of being.

"What are you to me, woman?" he rasped, powerful fingers still sifting through the softness at the apex of her thighs. He could run his fingers through her curls all day — a simple but serene pleasure in a world where fate was anything but.

He sighed as he stared down at her. He might not be able to mesmerize her, but he grimly conceded that she wielded that power over him.

"I still needs bring you to heel, Alexandria."

The future was ambiguous, the destiny of the war's end unknown. All that Malik could do was follow the instinct inside of him, the primitive impulse that made him desirous of keeping Alexandria the Great as close to him as possible.

* * * * *

"You're going the wrong way."

Fija stilled, immediately recognizing the voice. She slowly turned on her heel until at last she faced him. She realized her warriors were shocked when she deigned to speak to him. "And what would a male know, hm?"

The warriors of Zala had spent the last two days preparing to journey the black waters. In the end, Fija had decided she would trust the task of rescuing the queen to none but herself. Choosing but five of her strongest, deadliest entourage to accompany her, she knew that taking too many would give the wrong result.

The Takuri were not prepared to wage all-out war on the demons. Not yet. At this juncture, she felt it prudent to go in quietly, get back their queen, and return to the fortress. Once Alexandria the Great was safe...then and only then would they ready their troops for the final, deciding battle.

The black-skinned male raised an arrogant eyebrow. Fija found the affectation at once arousing and annoying.

"If you believe she is your queen, then you must believe the story she told you...specifically the story of where she—*we*—came from." Another damned eyebrow inched up. "We know where Tongor is. You do not."

Fija's nostrils flared, but she said nothing.

"So the way we see it," another male, the one called John intoned, "is we can work together or we can work apart. Either way, you're heading in the wrong direction."

Surely this was a cruel joke of the gods, Fija thought on a sigh. The last thing any of her warriors needed, herself included, was the distraction of these males. Yet, perversely, their logic could not be refuted.

"Well?" Peacock drawled, looking irritatingly bored. "What will it be, sweet thang?"

Fija looked back to her trusted warriors. They frowned, but shuffled their gazes to the ground. Tilting her head back to face Peacock, she gritted out, "Fine. But you needs must stay out of my way."

* * * * *

Alex awoke on a whimper, her body weak. She couldn't open her eyes no matter how hard she tried. Every muscle seemed to groan, protesting its use as she stretched. She felt as though she'd been run over by one of those super high-speed automated glider-cabs that used to shuffle her to and from her office at NASA every day.

Sounds assaulted her. Laughter. Happiness. Boisterous clamor. The fact that those same sounds pierced her skull like a knife served as her first coherent reminder that she was on the mend. But healing from what?

She had been ill…that much she remembered with crystal clarity. But why? How? What had caused—

Alex stilled as memories returned. The dungeon. The cage. No food or water…

Her eyes flew open, the abrupt movement nauseating in the extreme. She groaned, her eyelids batting in rapid succession as she fought with her pupils to adjust to the light—and with her stomach to keep from expelling itself.

"She awakens," Alex heard a female whisper.

"We needs must inform His Greatness," another said.

"I shall notify him," a male voice gruffly answered. "The deuce of you see to your duties."

Heavy footfalls walked further and further away. Alex's eyes adjusted to the softly lit atmosphere just in time to watch a male dressed in a thigh-high leather skirt and matching black boots disappear into an adjoining corridor.

Her gaze flicked up to where two naked females hovered, standing over her all but lifeless body. They stood there looking down at her with a tranquility as serene, beautiful, and complacent as two china dolls in a window display.

She frowned. There was something strange about those two.

The eyes. Alex's forehead wrinkled as it occurred to her that their eyes looked...wrong. The irises were light silver, almost opaque. But that wasn't the strange part in this already too-strange world. What chilled her was the fact that their gazes lacked life. They resembled programmed droids, but something told her they were very, very human.

Not Xandi females — *Takuri* females.

"I-I'm thirsty," Alex whispered, her underused voice gravelly. "Help me."

Their smiles never wavered. "King Malik will see to your needs," one doll cheerfully informed her. "As you will see to his."

"Are you Takuri?"

Still, the smiles.

"My sister and I were born lowly humans, but have found redemption in the beds of the masters we serve." Doll number one inclined her head towards doll number two. The smiles remained hauntingly luminous. "I am Mara and this is Anya. We are here to welcome you to your new home and new life."

Greeeeat. Just what Alex had been hoping to wake up to. The Tongor version of the Stepford welcome wagon.

"You welcomed me," Alex growled. "Job well done. Now leave!" she barked. She began to cough, the guttural sound she'd issued too much for her throat to endure.

"We cannot leave until one superior to ourselves permits us to do thusly."

Kill the fucking smiles already!

Alex's eyes narrowed. "Who is superior to you?" she asked between coughs.

"Any male," said Mara.

"Any male *Xandi*," Anya clarified.

"But we needs must listen to only our masters and the awakened king-god," Mara chimed in.

Alex's teeth gritted. She'd been snatched from a world of matriarchal madness and thrown into a world of patriarchal insanity. She didn't know which was worse, only that she didn't want to end up a mindless, thoughtless doll like Frick and Frack. For that reason, they were simply too horrifying to look at.

"Get," she said distinctly, over-enunciating every word, "away from me." When they made no move to leave, just stood there like two smiling idiots, Alex forced herself to her feet. They were giving her a major case of the creeps. "I said go away!" She coughed, but stalked towards them. "Now! I said—*umph*."

A sudden and powerful choking sensation forced Alex to stop in her tracks. Her eyes bulged as she gasped and sputtered for air; her hands flew up to her throat.

Bastard. The son of a bitch had put a collar around her neck.

Angry, humiliated, and undeniably shocked, Alex looked down and surveyed herself. She was naked, wearing a collar, and the collar was attached to a chain. Picking up a portion of the lightweight but surprisingly invulnerable chain, she slowly wound around in a circle until she found where the chain led to.

She stilled. The lead had been secured to a post. She, captain and commander of the *Methuselah*, had been reduced to the status of an exotic sex pet. Her heart sank, hopelessness and semi-hysteria seizing her.

Where is my crew? Please! Please don't leave me here!

Alex took a deep breath and slowly expelled it. She battled with her fraught emotions, refusing to succumb to them. She knew the crew would come for her. It was just a matter of finding her. Peacock, Vlad, and John would keep their promise.

Get it together, Doctor. This will end soon. Don't let them break you.

"Mara! Anya!" an all too familiar male voice boomed. "Your masters await you. Depart."

The dolls bowed and walked off with those serene smiles still plastered on their faces. Alex's eyes narrowed as her light green gaze darted from their retreating naked butts up into the face of the mammoth black reptile king.

"Why didn't you just kill me?" she asked, her voice still raspy. "I'd rather be dead than end up like those two."

"They are quite happy," Malik assured her. "They live to fulfill the every sexual and physical need of their respective master*sss*." His gold-slit gaze raked over her naked body. "Just as you will live to fulfill your king-god's every sexual and physical desire."

"They are 'happy', if one can stretch the meaning of the word far enough to accommodate the situation, because your people have robbed them of all thinking processes."

He shrugged. "And yet are they happy."

Alex's smile was anything but kind. "What's the problem? Aren't the men of your race strong enough to deal with women who can think?" Watching his nostrils flare, she enjoyed the knowledge she was irritating him. "Afraid the little girlies might say something to make the big, bad Xandis cry?"

"Enough!" he bellowed, slashing a hand through the air. He leaned in close, his reptilian face a breath away from hers. The sight of his predator's teeth made her heart pound. "Your words are treasonous and I should punish you for them."

"What will you do?" she whispered back, her gaze locked challengingly with his. She refused to show the fear she felt. "Starve me? Not give me water? Hmmm...that's scary," she taunted. "Never happened to me before."

"Little girl," he murmured, "one day you will push me too far." He stood up, looming over her with ten-and-a-half-feet and probably six hundred pounds of deadly, ripped muscle. "You needs must learn to listen."

Alex shook her head on a sigh. "Your people are as sick and depraved as the Takuri. The humans enslave men, the Xandi enslave women. I'd say you deserve each other." She gave him her back and walked toward the post she'd been hitched to. "But since I belong to neither race, I just want out of this nightmare."

Silence.

"If you are not Takuri," the deep, male voice murmured, "then what species are you?"

She sighed like a martyr. "You wouldn't believe me even if I told you."

"Tell me. I command you."

Alex cocked her head to look at him. Her gaze raked over his serious features. "I don't respond well to threats."

She could have sworn she heard the beast sigh. Oddly charming.

His jaw tightened. "Tell me. *Please*," he gruffly added.

"Unchain me," she said softly, "and I just might."

His smile was as grating to her as hers had been to him. "Not a chance."

CHAPTER SIXTEEN

Malik had made certain that the mesmerized females were the first sights Alexandria encountered upon waking in order to give her a mild taste of what life was like for domesticated Takuri females in Tongor. Human women were captured by their mates, collared and hypnotized until they were impregnated, and then fully mated and mesmerized. They lived out the remainder of their days in peaceful bliss with their respective masters, wanting for naught and cherished by their husbands.

He had shown Alexandria the mesmerized females even while knowing that the mortal queen was, herself, unable to be mesmerized. Malik had hoped she would see the beauty of the symbiotic relationship; understand that the Takuri were not harmed by Xandi males, merely tamed.

Apparently, the human queen was unmoved by such a notion.

Malik walked out onto the private balcony of his bedchamber and breathed in the purity of the red-tinted air. From his position above he could see some of the kingdom below that he would forever rule.

Simple homes of commoners which had been crafted from red clay and black earth and were nestled in circular precision around the palace. The larger, more expensive gold and metallic dwellings of the Xandi warriors which were positioned in circular precision around the commoners. The death pits beyond the homes of the warriors—black holes in the earth where heretics were offered down to the *loma* as meals.

Everything was as it should be. Everything was as it had been for thousands upon thousands of years.

This woman, this so-called Alexandria the Great, dare mocked all that Malik had been raised to believe was superior and just. One-thousand-four-hundred-twenty-six years ago, he had been born to a mortal Xandi sire from the womb of a mortal, mesmerized, Takuri mother. She had lived out her years in the very happy, sublime state the human queen scoffed at.

Malik's muscles tensed as he stared at nothing, his gaze absently raking over the world he had vowed to protect from the time he was old enough to understand the scope of the twenty thousand years-long war that had raged on—and the impact it had on his race. Alexandria was not the first Takuri to balk at the sight of a mesmerized female. The only difference between her and the thousands before her was the fact that, even though she didn't yet realize it and perhaps feared a similar fate, she was incapable of being forced into a symbiotic relationship.

She had to choose it.

He took a deep breath in and slowly exhaled. One way or another he would bring her to heel. She *would* come to see the Xandi way of life as superior. The prophesized queen of humans *would* bow down before him...not just physically, but mentally as well.

By immobilizing Alexandria the Great, Malik took away the Takuri's sole symbol of hope. Without her intervention and determination, their spirits would dampen and they would, at long last, be forced under Xandi dominion. Such was the way of nature.

Such was destiny.

Malik clenched and released his fist. He had endured more battles with the *lomu* and other lower orders of predators than he could name, yet never had he felt such tension consume him as this. For the first time in his mortal and immortal lives, he didn't know where to begin or how to proceed. All that he did know was it *had* to be accomplished. There was too much at stake for failure.

"You will be mine, Alexandria," he murmured. Coal-black hair threaded with golden highlights whipped in the wind. Serpentine-gold eyes narrowed in concentration, determination. "One way or another, you will be mine."

* * * * *

Naked, Alex was led by her collar down a long, ornate corridor. Her eyes widened as she took in the architecture, immediately noting the resemblance between Xandi art and artifacts that would have been found in ancient Egypt. Too weird. Whomever had said that history repeats itself had said a mouthful. The Takuri civilization rivaled ancient Greece and the Xandi civilization was a throwback to dead Egypt.

Malik held the lead to the chain that kept her bound to him. She had seen other black, winged, reptilian creatures shift into man-like forms, but she'd never seen their king do so. She wondered if he was capable of it or if his beast form was an immobile one. And if he *was* capable of shape-shifting, she wondered why he had never done so in her presence.

The other form she'd seen various Xandi take on, the humanesque one, was very similar to Takuri males. Xandi men were built a bit taller and more inherently muscular, but from the neck down they otherwise looked like any other human. It was just the face that was different.

Xandi faces reminded Alex of fabled vampires. Their expressions were intensely brooding, their incisors were undeniably fangs, and the pupils of their eyes were slit like snakes while the irises remained gold no matter what form they took on.

Those were the differences. In all other physical aspects, they could have passed for Takuri.

The sound of boisterous laughter startled Alex out of her reverie. She tensed up when Malik led her into a dining hall, her nudity there for all to see. Approximately forty people were situated around one long table, twenty Xandi males and twenty of those brainwashed females. The women, like her, were all naked. The men, unlike the nude black reptile holding her chain, were dressed in thigh-high leather skirts of various hues and matching leather knee-high boots. All of them stood up when their king approached.

"Great One," they murmured in unison.

Malik nodded and they sat down. The scent of food reached Alex's nostrils, making her belly rumble. Her captor glanced back, looking pointedly at her stomach and then into her eyes. He leaned his reptilian face in close to hers and murmured, "Do you show them your obedience to me, you will eat."

She frowned, but said nothing. She wasn't certain she understood how she was to show her obedience, and she deeply suspected she didn't want to find out, but sweet God did her belly want food. Unlike the main entrée in Zala, roasted fish tongue, this smorgasbord of treats actually looked and smelled good. Her mouth began to water.

Malik took his ornamental seat at the head of the table. The chair was red and quite large, big enough to support the weight of a creature his size. Alex made a move to sit in the unoccupied and far less ostentatious seat next to his, but he yanked at the chain.

"Before you are permitted to sit at the same table with these *civilized* females," he announced, making her teeth grind together, "you must demonstrate your willingness to please your king-god."

Alex looked at Malik hesitantly. She wasn't in the mood for a war of the wills. She was tired, she was hungry, and she needed sustenance badly. Unless he wanted her to rip out someone's heart and eat it, or some other God-awful ritual, she prepared herself to do as he said. For now.

"Sit up on the table in front of me," he ordered. "Then lie on your back and spread your legs."

Her heart began to pound. She hadn't been prepared for a show like *that*. Would he choose this moment for their first penetration? In front of forty of his people? Her face flushed with humiliation at the mere thought.

All eyes were on her. She glanced away from Malik, but could feel his stare still on her. She looked at the food, then away from it. Then back to the food, then away again. She must have repeated the action a dozen or so times before finally deciding that, come what may, she was going to eat. Alex consoled herself with the knowledge that she had to be healthy when her crew arrived to rescue her or it would be difficult on them to get her out of here.

Be strong, Commander Frazier. Don't let this break you.

Doing as she'd been instructed, Alex hopped up on the table in front of Malik. His men began to cheer and laugh as she lay down on her back and spread her legs. Fire suffused her cheeks, but otherwise she betrayed no emotion.

"Beg me," he said thickly. "Beg your king-god to taste your cream."

The men laughed louder. Alex's cheeks burned brighter. She ignored her embarrassment and concentrated on the objective—food.

"Please..." she said softly, "please taste my cream."

A reptilian finger found one of her nipples and began to toy with it, gently rolling it from side to side until it stood hard and stiff. She hated that the damn thing grew erect for him, but realized it couldn't be helped when he was purposely playing with it.

"*Hmmm...*" Malik purred, a deep sound that reverberated in the back of his throat, "You have a pretty cunt, but you've been a very disobedient little girl. You don't deserve for your king-god to touch you let alone taste you."

The scent of food was powerfully intoxicating. "*Please,*" Alex said with more force. She just had to eat. If it meant being Pavlov's dog until her crew rescued her from these monsters, then so be it. She'd survived worse. "Please taste my—your—cream."

Silence ensued. Her belly rumbled mercilessly.

She knew he was appeased when a forked tongue snaked out and began licking the folds of her vagina. Murmurs of approval filled the dining chamber, congratulating the king on bringing the human to heel so quickly. The words grated, so she ignored them.

His tongue found her hole and penetrated it. She whimpered just a bit as he began to stroke in and out of her, soft, almost sensuous movements that caused an unwanted ball of arousal to knot in her belly. He kept the pace slow and steady—too slow to come, too fast not to grow wet.

She blocked out the sounds of the continual murmurings and chuckles being elicited by the Xandi around her. The ache in her stomach grew and grew. One second the king's tongue was grinding away inside of her and a blink of an eye later he had withdrew it.

Alex gasped when Malik's forked tongue curled around her clit and began to suckle. Her hips instinctively flared up, her nipples stabbing high into the air. Those reptilian fingers found her nipples, gently tugging and pulling at them while he licked and sucked on her flesh. She moaned, unable to stop the small sound before it came out.

He sucked on her pussy hard, making her entire body writhe and shake. Her breasts heaved up and down from below his knowing palms as her body steeled itself to come. Relentlessly suckling her clit, the king tugged at her nipples harder.

"Oh God."

Alex popped, groaning as the knot of arousal in her belly exploded. She came hard and furiously, giving him the cream he'd demanded of her. "Oh God," she moaned again as she convulsed, her entire body shaking.

He lapped up her juices, a purr in the back of his throat as he sucked on her hole. When he was done and apparently satiated his bald head rose from between her thighs.

"Oh king-god," Malik said.

She blinked.

"You said 'oh god', but the proper address to me," he arrogantly corrected her, "is 'king-god'."

Her nostrils flared as their gazes met. "May I sit on the chair and eat now?"

Silence.

And then, slowly and with irritating pompousness, Malik waved a hand toward the chair next to his. "My good little girl may eat now."

"Thank you," she ground out.

* * * * *

The same ritual was repeated twice daily, at morning and in the evening, for an entire week. A hungry Alex was led into the dining chamber, she climbed up onto the table and came for the king before his men, and then she was permitted to sit next to him and eat food out of his hand. She wouldn't be allowed to eat "like a big girl" by herself until she was totally broken and compliant, or what Malik liked to call "civilized".

Other than at meals, he made no move to touch her. She didn't see much of him—only at breakfast, dinner, and when it was time to go to sleep. He kept her next to him in his huge bed all through the night, the lead to her chain firmly in his powerful grasp, but other than lying close to her, he didn't touch, let alone rape her.

For some reason, perhaps because of the dreams she'd been plagued with, that surprised Alex. She could tell he wanted inside of her—all the signs were there. He might be of a different species, but Alex was learning that males were males. His eyes grew heavy-lidded when she was near him, his penis was always erect, yet he never did anything about it. The only time he sexually recognized her was at meals.

By the end of the first week, Alex automatically went up on the table without prompting. She no longer winced at the perceived humiliation or felt frightened by his touch. After a few days more of this, however, the king upped the proverbial ante.

"I have been kind to you," Malik said as she ate from the palm of his hand. He sounded almost bored. "I have nourished you even though you have failed to demonstrate your appreciation for all that I am and all that I do."

She glanced up and eyed him curiously. She'd done exactly as he'd wanted every day, in exactly the fashion she'd been told to do. She let the servants bathe her, shave her pubic hair, and keep her body slicked down with exotic-smelling oils without a fight. She hopped up on the table before every meal and allowed him to have his wicked way with her without an argument. She slept in his bed beside him at night like a compliant doll. *Fail him?*

"Show your appreciation of this meal in a way becoming a woman."

Alex's forehead crinkled. She had no idea what he was talking about.

He sighed as though she was a simpleton. "Alexandria," the king said loudly before the assembled men and their doll-wives.

"Yes?"

"My cock is hard. Get on your knees and suckle it until I give you my cream."

She stilled. Her pulse went through the roof. They'd never had intercourse, but she'd felt his erection pressed against her backside every night since she'd been taken from the cage. He might not have penetrated her, but his penis was always swollen and ready. Because of that fact she knew just how big it was—

Too big.

But that was a trite issue compared to the major one. It was one thing for him to touch her—she could let her mind drift off to another place—but it was another thing entirely for her to touch him. He probably knew that, too.

"Well?" he hissed, as arrogant as ever.

Alex inwardly debated for a long moment. Her hands twisted in her lap. If she complied, she was taking the experiment of Pavlov's dog to a new extreme. If she failed to comply, he might very well deny her breakfast tomorrow morning. As is, he fed her but twice a day—just enough to make certain she'd have hunger pangs in time for the next meal.

Conceding that she had little choice, Alex rose from her seat. She wanted to smack the portentous expression off his face; right now all she could do was daydream about doing it.

"Alexandria is my good little girl this eve," he murmured. "Now kneel before me and take my cock into your mouth. My balls are sensitive so treat them as the treasures they are."

How about if I bite one of them off? Is that sensitive enough for you?

Her jaw tightened. "Yes, my king-god," Alex grated. She was beginning to get the sinking feeling that her crew would never find her.

And that escape was up to her.

Alex put all thoughts of her crew and being rescued from her mind as she kneeled before the ever-demanding king. She needed to concentrate on the here and now, on getting the food her body needed so that, come what may, she was prepared for whatever fate threw her — rescue or escape.

She took her first good look at his naked, swollen cock. She sighed in relief when she realized it was vulnerably smooth, like a man's. It was possessed of more ridges, but otherwise the same. The thought of trying to give a blowjob to a reptilian cock had been decidedly unpleasant. This was at least bearable.

On edge, Alex tentatively licked the crown of his big head. Malik hissed, letting her know that he liked it. Her jaw muscles relaxed a bit at the sound and, taking a deep breath, she popped the entire head into the warmth and wetness of her mouth. Immediately, she felt his thigh muscles tense. She began to suck slowly — only the head.

"You look to be enjoying yourself, Great One," a male laughed.

"Hmmm," she heard Malik taunt. "It feels all right, but my Xandi female servants are better at it."

Alex's nostrils flared. For some insane reason, the insult smarted.

All right, bastard. You want it, you got it…

She pressed his cock into her depths, deep-throating him in one smooth motion. He hissed, his sharp claws threading through her hair and holding her face up against his manhood. She sucked hard on his length and retreated at the same time, giving herself some air and him a moan he couldn't help but to elicit. Feeling vastly indignant, and a little dumb for caring, she repeated the movements — smooth glide in, hard suck on the retreat, smooth glide in, hard suck on the retreat.

"Faster," he said thickly.

Alex reached up and began to gently knead his balls, turning his moan into a deadly growl that rumbled low in his throat. She worked her mouth faster then, sucking his cock frenziedly. Her head bobbed up and down in a frenetic motion, sucking sounds penetrating the quiet of the dining chamber.

Every muscle in his gargantuan body tensed. His palms rested at either side of her face, the deadly pikes he called fingernails keeping her golden hair out of his line of vision.

She knew he was watching his black cock disappear into her mouth, knew too that he loved what he saw. She sucked him and sucked him, over and over, again and again.

Alex kept kneading his balls as she brought him to the edge. Figuring out that his left one was more sensitive than his right one, she expertly rolled it around while her lips and tongue worked their magic on his cock. She sucked harder and faster, mercilessly enveloping him again and again and—

Malik's body stiffened as he came on a loud groan. Hot cum spurted into her mouth, hitting the back of her throat. His fingers tightened in her hair as he moaned out his pleasure. She swallowed his cum in a single gulp.

Her breathing as heavy as his, Alex slowly released his semi-erect cock and looked up. Their gazes met and locked. He tasted...different from a man. And, as loath as she was to admit it, the different was better.

What are you thinking? You're going crazy! There is nothing about this beast that is better than a man. Nothing!

Alex tore her gaze from his. Touching him *had* been different from when he touched her. When she was forced to pay him attention, she couldn't disassociate. She had touched others before and felt nothing. There had even been some sexual encounters with Robert where he had been in the mood, she hadn't, but she had gone through the motions to please him...and felt nothing.

With Malik she couldn't shut down. Somehow she had known that would happen. He had spent months haunting her dreams and now he was trying to haunt her every waking moment.

She stood up on two shaky feet and snatched the lead to the chain from his grasp. "I need to be alone," she said quietly.

Alex sprinted from the dining chamber as fast as her feet would carry her. She could feel his serpentine-gold eyes on her back as he watched her run away.

CHAPTER SEVENTEEN

She was asleep.

Malik lay next to Alexandria in his palatial harem bed, his eyes on her naked buttocks. He could see the folds of her pretty pink pussy tucked neatly below them and wanted to impale her more than words could say.

This was the very bed that, in his mortal life, he had fucked Xandi females in left and right. Sometimes three or four of them at a time. Sometimes ten to twenty of them at a time. Yet now, in his immortal life, the only female he craved to be inside was the one lying next to him.

The only one in his world of privilege and power who didn't want him.

He reached out a hand so as not to awaken her and sifted through her beautiful, long, golden hair. Like the foreign pinkness of her nipples, it was the most remarkable and erotic color.

"What are you to me?" he murmured, not wanting to wake her. He didn't show vulnerability to any creature, let alone to the very woman who loathed him. "You haunted me in the dreamstate. You make me feel...things...now."

Sighing, Malik traced a path from her hair, down her shoulder, and onward to her right hip. He let his palm rest there, absently stroking her hip, thigh, and belly as he submerged himself in his thoughts.

Every day he grew closer to breaking her will whether she realized it or not. Every day she relented just a little bit more. For the first time he wondered if that was what he wanted. This eve she had suckled his cock not because she wanted to, but because she'd had to. With any other female he wouldn't have cared. With this one…

He wanted her to want him.

They made no sense, these feelings. And because they were as foreign to him as the colors which decorated her body, it was difficult to discern why they were there. He'd never felt like this before. He'd never felt before, period. Emotions were for the weak and got you killed.

"Sleep well," Malik said in low tones. He continued to stroke her hip, thigh, and belly. "Sleep in peace."

Alex feigned sleep while her mind worked a mile a minute. She had never felt so keyed up or on the edge of losing it in her entire life.

She'd heard his words. She'd recognized the inherent confusion in them.

It was exactly how she felt.

What were they to each other? Malik had mentioned a dreamstate — apparently the dreams she'd had of him…they'd shared them together? This made no sense. And yet she was certain she'd heard him say that very thing.

Fija had spoken of destinies and prophecies, of an Alexandria the Great of Methuselah who was to lead the Takuri from bondage and fear to a world free of those restraints. What if she was right? What if, as insane as it had sounded at the time Fija had said she was the one, Alex *was* that prophesized leader? Weirder things had happened as of late.

If it was true, she thought with a heavy heart, then it could very well be her destiny to slay the dragon lying next to her in the bed. It was easier to slay the dragon you didn't know than the one who kept you warm every night.

It was easier to make war on evil than on a creature who, in the "dreamstate", you had grown to care for.

Unfortunately, it wasn't just in the dreamstate. She was growing to care for him out of it, too. For all his bluster, he had been shockingly kind to her these past couple of weeks. Gentle, even. Forcing her at dinner to recognize that he was there, to touch him and bring him to climax, had only brought all kinds of crazy emotions bubbling to the surface.

Feelings that had been there already. Feelings that had been dormant, but real nevertheless.

She had spent months with him in the nighttime before they'd met in the flesh. So much time that she had more or less been able to anticipate his every move once the dreams had become reality. They had shared a connection there just as they shared an inexplicable one here.

Alex's eyes flicked open in the darkness. She stared at nothing as she lay there, the feel of his reptilian hand gently stroking her hip, thigh, and belly provoking carnal sensations inside of her that she'd rather not experience.

You could roll over and offer yourself to him. What would it hurt? Just one time...

Closing her eyes, she vowed to fight the bizarre need she felt to be as close to him as possible. If there was such a thing as fate, Alex didn't want to become any more emotionally entwined with the enemy than what she already was.

* * * * *

"It's got to be this way."

"You are certain?"

"No. But I'm as sure as I can be."

"We don't have time for mistakes, male! If you're not certain then—"

Vlad blocked out the familiar sound of Fija and Peacock arguing and concentrated on the gauge he was holding in his hand. Other than munitions, it was the only piece of equipment he'd managed to salvage from the body of *Methuselah II*—an aircraft that had presumably been blown to bits with the sea predator.

The gauge had been small enough to slip into his pocket, so Vlad had taken it. What it was now saying made no sense at all. Concentrating on the tiny, highly advanced machine in his hand, he did a quick check to make sure there was no malfunction.

It was operating correctly. He swallowed heavily.

"Hey!" John shouted, gaining everyone's attention. "Would you two stop fighting already! It's getting on my nerves!"

A female warrior harrumphed in such a way to let everyone know she agreed. Fija glanced up at her, scowled, then relented.

"Let us go," the Amazon barked. "And let us hope the male knows what he is about."

Vlad used the back of his hand to swipe perspiration from his brow. For now he would keep what information he'd just acquired to himself.

The machine was malfunctioning. It had to be.

PART IV:
INTO THE DARKNESS

CHAPTER EIGHTEEN

After bathing in water and being vigorously scrubbed down by soap and sponge, Alex was placed in a second bath, this one enriched with sweet-scented oils. There her pubic hair was shaved and oils worked into her skin. Following that morning ritual, she was led by three bathing servants back into the elaborate suite decorated of reds and golds where she spent most of her time.

Usually the king was waiting for her there so he could take her to breakfast. This morning he was not. She prayed that didn't mean what she thought it meant, namely that she wasn't permitted to eat. Her belly was rumbling something fierce.

On the cusp of working herself up into a fit of anger, Alex stilled when she noticed an ornate gold and bejeweled table on the far side of the bedchamber. There was a single chair pushed up against it and it was loaded down with all sorts of scrumptious looking foods. Her mouth began to water, hunger pangs assaulting her.

"For you," one of the Xandi bathing servants told her. Handing Alex the lead to her chain, she motioned toward the table. "The king-god does permit you to eat in solitude this morn."

Alex was stunned, but appreciative. She inclined her head toward the servant before scurrying off to eat to her heart's content. She wasted no time gobbling down everything she wanted, her favorites being the sweet bread and yam-like vegetables that were part and parcel of every breakfast in Tongor.

Satiated, she sat back and reflected on what had once been an uncomplicated pleasure — eating what she wanted, how much of it she wanted, and doing so in privacy. She had no idea why Malik had given her this simple gift, but was grateful for it.

A few minutes later, a ripple of awareness passed through Alex, a sensation that let her know she was being watched. The presence was a familiar one.

"Good morning," Alex said without turning around.

Silence.

"How did you know I was here?" His voice was deep…and convincingly surprised.

She shrugged. "I seem to know a lot about you, just as you seem to know a lot about me. What I don't understand is how. Or why."

"What manner of creature are you?" he murmured.

Alex smiled. He was coming straight to the point. Turning around, she took her first look of the day at Malik. There was no change in his ferocious-looking, reptilian appearance, but a major change in his eyes. He looked as confused as she felt. "The truth?"

"Of course."

She sighed, her smile evaporating. He had come straight to the point, so she might as well, too. "I'm over one hundred million years old."

He stilled, but betrayed no emotion.

"I suppose you could call me a human, but if so I'm an ancient one. That's why I am physically different from the Takuri."

Still he said nothing, so Alex went on. She told him where she had been born, about her career with NASA and the deep-space mission, about the cryptic warning the *Methuselah* had received from Earth, and about how a nuclear explosion had managed to send her crew reeling through the annals of time and space. At her tale's conclusion, she was well aware of the fact she had an enraptured one-king audience inching closer and closer to her.

"This is much to accept as the truth."

"Yes. I know."

"And yet do I believe you."

Her shoulders straightened. She nodded, thankful to him for simply believing...and not taking her through all the motions that Fija had.

"Perhaps you are not Takuri," he rumbled out, "yet you are their prophesized queen."

Their gazes met and locked.

"The Takuri believe that to be true. But if you believe that," Alex said softly, "then why do you keep me alive?"

Again, silence.

Finally, one side of his mouth hitched up in a small smile. "I do not know," Malik admitted.

There was something between them, some inexplicable thing that neither of them could understand. They didn't want for it to be there, but staring at each other only made it more obvious that the connection did, in fact, exist.

Alex's eyelids grew heavy when she saw his swollen erection jutting out from his groin. Arousal knotted in her belly.

"I am your enemy," she whispered, standing up.

"Yes." He walked a bit closer, the wings on his back expanding. "You are."

Her breasts were heaving up and down, her nipples stiff and tight. "I could never be happy in your world."

"You cannot say that with all certainty." He drew nearer.

"I have thoughts and feelings and needs."

"I know." And nearer.

"I am not a doll like those other Takuri whose minds you have stolen."

Malik said nothing, just walked closer and closer to where she stood, her body naked and trembling.

By the time he stood before her, towering over her frame by double the measurement, the arousal inside of her was a merciless knot of tension and desire. He ran one black reptile's hand down her neck and then lower to cover her breast. Flicking her hard nipple back and forth with his thumb, all she could do was shudder in response.

"You want me to want you."

"I do," Malik murmured.

Torn between arousal and fear of the unknown, Alex hesitated for a long moment. Out of all the crazy things that had happened to her since disembarking on Earth in the year 100,000,007, what she was contemplating doing next was the craziest.

She'd never been with any man except for Robert. Married straight out of high school, they had been together her entire adult life. Other than her dead husband, there had only been one emotionless droid that had ever touched her. He—it—was dead, too. And now here she stood, preparing to join bodies with a male that wasn't of her own species, or even close to it.

But he made her *feel*, damn it. He made her feel and that was something she had never thought to know again. He sparked a sense of need and knowing inside of her she'd never before experienced...not even with Robert.

Making her decision, she held out a trembling right hand and tentatively squeezed his cock. His answering hiss was her undoing.

"I want you," she admitted, swallowing heavily. "I'm afraid, but I want to be with you. Just once."

His smile was typical Malik arrogance. "You'll want me more than once."

A blink later, Alex found herself being forcefully, but reverently, thrown onto the plush harem bed. Another second and her knees were thrust apart, his gigantic body situated intimately between them.

"I know not what you are to me, Alexandria," he rasped out, "but I need to be inside you."

Alex felt a moment's fear as she took in the sight before her. Positing himself between her legs and guiding his huge cock towards her small opening was the ten-and-a-half-feet-tall genetic cross between a gargoyle and a black lizard. When his bald head came up and those gold-slit eyes were revealed to her, the coil of tension in her belly responded to the obvious desire she saw in them.

He looked as entranced by her as she was by him.

"I don't know what you are to me, either," Alex whispered, "but I want you to fuck me."

Malik's jaw tightened at her provocative words. Their gazes met and held as he positioned the head of his thick cock at her cunt. He'd been wanting this moment to happen ever since his awakening. He'd desired none other but Alexandria, the need to be close to her overwhelming in its intensity. And now she lay before him, compliant and willing.

Her long, golden curls fanned out beneath her, stunning in their beauty. Her hard nipples jutted up, beckoning to his mouth and hands. Her pussy was as pink and swollen as her nipples, the hole small and tight.

Later he would take his time. Later he would spend hour upon hour licking every inch of her. Right now, he decided on a clenched jaw, he just needed to join with her.

Malik impaled her on a low, resonating groan, his eyelids heavy as he pressed his cock deep inside her. Alexandria moaned in response, her back arching and her nipples stabbing up even higher into the air.

She felt so good. So damn tight and warm.

"Malik..."

He knew what she wanted. It was what he wanted, too.

Wasting no time with the preliminaries—no foreplay, no more words, no nothing—he gave her the hard, merciless fuck they both craved. Palming her breasts and massaging her stiff nipples, he began to rock in and out of her, pounding away inside of her cunt. He moaned as he fucked her, having never felt a pussy that pulled him back in with every outstroke. But then this was Alexandria...

Everything about her was exotic. Everything about her was perfect.

Malik took her harder, his hands at her knees, holding them far apart. A growl threatening to rumble from low in his throat, he tried to hold it back for fear of frightening her. Luckily it didn't faze her, for he didn't succeed.

On a loud, territorial growl, Malik impaled her over and over, again and again and again. The sound of her flesh enveloping his echoed throughout the bedchamber. The tangy scent of their combined arousal perfumed the air about them.

"Harder," she gritted out, her nostrils flaring, "*please.*"

They stared at each other the entire time, their gazes never wavering as he gave her what she wanted. He rode her cunt hard, fucking her with the ruthlessness of his species. In and out, harder, faster, deeper—

"*Malik.*" Her eyes rolled back into her head and she screamed, telling him without words she had found her pleasure. Her pussy began to quiver in a series of foreign contractions—another surprise—and before he could stop himself he had passed the edge from which there was no turning back.

Malik plunged in and out of her cunt once, twice, three times more. On the loudest, fiercest roar his throat had ever issued, he threw his head back and came fast and hard. He spurted semen deep inside of her, the volcanic feeling one he wish could go on and on forever.

Alex's eyes widened as she watched him shape-shift before her eyes. One moment he had been a beast and then, a moment later when he roared and his body stiffened atop hers as he came, his entire being morphed into that of a man.

She watched in fascination and awe as he regained some control of himself and, not bothering to shift back into beast form, looked down at her through the gold eyes of his race.

He was a beautiful vampire with his fanged incisors and intense expression. A more masculine and deadly face she'd never seen, but it was beautiful.

Neither of them said a word as he came down on top of her, their gazes still locked as if transfixed. They studied each other for a suspended moment before he closed his eyes and placed a single, gentle kiss on her forehead.

Her heart thumped in a way it never had before.

Alex said nothing when Malik laid down his head and found comfort between her breasts. She raised her hands and held him tight, not wanting to let go.

CHAPTER NINETEEN

On her back, a hand flung over her head, Alex awoke to the feel of her nipples being sucked. She moaned, her eyelids batting in rapid succession as she forced them open.

"Good morning," she breathed out, noting that he had remained in his man-like form. She smiled, reaching down and running her fingers through hair she hadn't known he possessed until he'd shifted last night. It was a sexy, shoulder-length, inky black with threads of gold woven through it.

He raised his eyebrows, gazing at her from beneath them. He smiled as best he could around her nipple, but didn't release it to return her greeting. She grinned.

Alex watched him suck on her nipples, arousal knotting in her belly. He sucked on one until it was stiff and hard, then switched to the other and did the same. Back and forth, over and over again.

Within minutes her expression had taken on a drugged look, her body writhing beneath his. "Please," she whispered, arching her back. "I want you inside me."

Malik raised his head from her chest. A light green gaze clashed with a serpentine gold one.

"Tell me," he said thickly, coming down on top of her. "I want to hear from your lips how badly you want your king-god to fuck you."

She frowned. "I have problems referring to any man as my king, let alone as my god."

Malik reached between her thighs and began stroking her clit in the way he knew she liked. Alex sucked in her breath.

"On the other hand," she demurred, "if the title fits…"

"Tell me," he again demanded. His voice was deep with authority and low with need.

"I want my king-god to fuck me," Alex whispered. She closed her eyes and moaned when the circles at her clit became more vigorous. *"Badly."*

"And I wish to fuck my queen-goddess."

Alex's eyes flew open. She had not been expecting him to refer to her in such an egalitarian way. The term, which would have sounded dumb coming from any man's lips but this one, squeezed her heart in the most pleasurable way.

For him, such a term carried a world of meaning.

There was something else she had not been expecting. Alex realized for the first time since she'd awoken that the chain had been removed from her. The thin, ornate, gold collar still decorated her neck, but there was no leash attached to it.

"Then do it." She raised her hips, arching them up to him. "Please."

His half-smile was arrogance personified. And very Malik.

"Roll over," he murmured. "I want to see your gorgeous ass jiggle when I fuck you."

Malik was carnal in a way she'd never known. The words were undeniably provocative, as was the mental image they conjured up. She waited for him to sit up on his knees and then, just like he wanted, rolled over onto her belly.

"All fours," Malik purred. "Ass and head both up. I want those sexy tits of yours to jiggle, too."

Alex blew out a breath. He was capable of igniting fire within her using no more than words. Again, she obeyed, taking to all fours, arching her back like a sleek cat.

He grabbed her hips and positioned his cock at her hole. The absence of pubic hair made every sensation increased by a hundredfold.

"Please, Malik," she said softly, wanting him more than she wanted to breathe. She wiggled her ass, letting him know she was more than eager and ready. "I want my king-god to fuck me."

A small, low growl began to reverberate in his chest. She smiled to herself, recognizing what that meant—he was about to fuck her brains out. Almost literally.

Malik impaled her from behind in one smooth thrust, seating himself to the hilt. She groaned long and loud, her smile evaporating and replaced with a serious, intense expression. Glancing over her shoulder, her eyes were narrowed in passion. "Fuck me."

His jaw clenched at her words. Giving her what she wanted, Malik began to pound in and out of her in long, fast, ruthless strokes. He moaned as he took her, his fingers digging into the flesh of her hips.

"I love my little girl's pussy," he purred, the sound as intoxicating as the rigorous impalements. "So wet and sticky and tight."

Alex's tits began to jiggle in time with his thrusts, her nipples super-sensitive from the rapid movements. "More," she begged. "*Harder.*"

"Like this?" he gritted out.

Grabbing her hips even tighter, he rode her hard, fucking her with branding, possessive strokes. The sound of perspiration-soaked flesh slapping perspiration-soaked flesh reached her ears. Harder. Faster. Again and again and again.

Alex threw her head back and groaned, a violent orgasm ripping from her belly. Blood rushed to her nipples, making them intensely sensitive. Blood rushed to her face, heating it. Her pussy contracted around his cock, the sound of his moans and her flesh suctioning his cock back inside of her all she could hear.

He growled in a familiar way that made her recognize he was close to climax. He took her impossibly harder, until she was keening with pleasure and begging for more. Alex threw her hips back at him, meeting him thrust for thrust. He took her harder—deeper—faster.

Over and over.

Again and again and again.

"Alexandria," he growled with an intensity she'd never before heard him use. *"You are mine,"* he said between thrusts. *"Forever are you bound to me."*

She felt his body stiffen, heard his loud growl, and knew he was about to explode. At the precise moment he did, his entire body convulsing, two sharp fangs sank into her neck, puncturing the skin and forcing her to scream.

The most ferocious orgasm Alex had ever experienced pummeled through her body like a bolt of lightning. She wailed even louder, the pleasure so intense as to be painful. He kept fucking her as he came, the sound of his loud growls rivaling her own screams. She continued to throw her hips back at him, milking his cock of its cream.

Malik squeezed her hips one last time before releasing them. His breathing labored, he fell onto the plush bed beside her and pulled her into his embrace. Alex gratefully collapsed on top of him, too spent to speak let alone remain awake.

* * * * *

Malik cradled Alexandria's sleeping body on his chest, his hands busy massaging her perfectly rounded buttocks. He was as exhausted as she was, but his mind was racing too mercilessly to slumber.

He had done the unthinkable. King Malik Ahmose had just given eternal life to the very woman the mages warned could be Tongor's ruin. Alexandria could no longer be killed, not that doing so had ever been an option, but he had taken things to an entirely new level by making her body as powerful as her unmesmerizable mind.

The human queen had no knowledge of what had passed between them when he'd bitten her. Of this he was certain. But soon, very soon, she would find out.

What are you to me, woman, that you make me so weak?

Malik sighed, wise enough to understand that there were some things not even the mages could predict. Like the affection he would feel towards the very female who had the power to bring his civilization to its knees.

* * * * *

Alex awoke in the middle of the night. She turned in the bed to face Malik, only to discover he wasn't there. Sitting up, she glanced around the bedchamber.

There he was...standing out on the balcony alone.

From this vantage point, King Malik Ahmose was every woman's fevered fantasy realized. Tall, broad, and chiseled out of impressive muscle, his seven-and-a-half-foot stature was as beautiful as it was deadly. His back and shoulders were broad and strong, his buttocks tight and perfect. His legs were long and neither too heavily nor too little muscled— just perfect. The manner in which the moonbeams spilled onto the balcony, highlighting his presence, made her believe that if there was such a thing as a king-god, Malik was surely him.

Scooting off the palatial bed, Alex quietly made her way towards where the Xandi king stood. The muscles in his back were tense. "Hey," she said softly, "are you okay?"

Silence ensued. She could tell something was very wrong so decided to patiently wait until he was ready to speak rather than prod him. Just when she thought he might never say a word, he slowly cocked his head to look down at her.

"Do you feel this...thing...between us? This inexplicable connection of sorts?"

Alex blew out a breath. More than he realized. "Yes."

"What does it mean?"

"I was kind of hoping you would know."

Malik glanced away. "I do not understand these feelings I have inside. Nor can I make sense of them."

Alex's smile was sad. It was almost as if they were the Romeo and Juliet of one hundred million years gone by. "'Deny thy father and refuse thy name'," she whispered.

His gaze darted back to hers, an eyebrow lifting inquisitively.

"I was quoting a silly play," Alex said on a sigh. "It's the tale of a man and a woman who long to be together despite the fact they were born enemies."

His expression was searching, sorrowful. "Then you do understand these feelings," he murmured.

"I do."

"What happened to this man and this woman?" he asked.

"They killed themselves. Both of them decided they would rather be dead than live out their lives apart."

Malik looked back out into the endless sea of black night. "Tragic."

"Hmmm…that's why that type of play was referred to as a 'tragedy'." Alex lifted her hand to his back and gently stroked him there. "But it wasn't real, Malik. It was only a tale."

"What future is there for us, Alexandria?" His dark-haired head whipped back around to regard her. "I am the leader of my people. You are the leader of yours. War has raged between our races for thousands of years. We are fools do we think to end it with a fuck or two."

The callous words stung. She looked away. "I guess you're right."

He lifted her chin with his hand until she met his gaze. "I did not mean that how it sounded, little one. I apologize."

Her heart swelled. Malik had never apologized to her before for anything. "Thank you," she whispered.

They threaded their hands together as they stood out on the balcony, both of them sucking the nighttime breeze into their lungs. It gave Alex time to think…and time to realize how much her presence here was hurting him. Whether or not he realized it at this moment in time, he would be happy again if she wasn't in Tongor.

I have grown to love you, King Malik Ahmose. This is why I am leaving. Because I love you enough to give you peace.

"Come on," Alex said softly, breaking the quiet. She squeezed his hand. "I want to make love with you tonight."

Malik hesitated for a brief moment, then followed her to the bed. He came down on top of her and entered her body with gentle reverence, thrusting slowly in and out of her welcoming flesh.

"No matter what fate brings to us," Malik promised in a whisper, "we will always live within the other."

Tears threatened to sting the backs of Alex's eyes. She smiled instead, realizing that she had to let him go. "I will always love you, Malik. Always."

Chapter Twenty

"I wish I had a machete," Peacock grumbled. "It would make cutting through this thick-ass shit a hell of a lot easier."

"I hear you, bro," John sighed, swiping at the sweat trickling down the side of his face.

Vlad kept his mouth shut and his eyes open as the men took the lead and made their way through the tropical forest. The female warriors stayed back, prepared to battle any predators that crossed their path.

"This disgusts me," Fija said acerbically to one of her warriors. "Tukuru is all but dying, our plant and animal life nigh unto nonexistent, while the barbaric Xandi revel in a world lush with vegetation."

"When we recapture our queen," one of the females reasonably pointed out, "we can claim this land for our own."

Vlad came to a halt. He turned around and stared at the Amazon. His eyes were big, wild. "You do not know this environment at all?" he rasped. "Or what sort of animals we are likely to encounter?"

Fija eyed him curiously. She glanced over to Peacock and John who were looking at him just as strangely. "No, I do not know it. Why do you question me thusly, male?"

"Vlad," Peacock murmured, "you're shaking, man."

"What's going on?" John asked. "You've been acting strange for days now."

"I-I—" Vlad took a deep breath and slowly exhaled. "At first I thought it was wrong—it had to be wrong!—but the further in-country we travel..."

"Vlad," John said softly, "you aren't making any sense. What had to be wrong? What are you talking about?"

Silence.

"I managed to salvage one of the devices from *Methuselah II*."

Peacock stilled. "Which one?"

Vlad was shaking like a leaf. "The d-date and t-time monitor."

Peacock shrugged. "Yeah. So?"

"It must have taken it time to realign itself. The reading we received upon landing was...inaccurate."

John's eyes narrowed. "How inaccurate?"

Vlad was given no time to answer. A horrifying roar echoed throughout the tropical terrain, gaining everyone's undivided attention. Impact tremors from massive footfalls caused everyone to fall to the ground. One second there had been nothing but huge trees as far as the eye could see. A second later, branches were snapping, trees were falling, and smaller animals were scurrying as the Terrible Lizard hunted its prey—

Them.

"Holy son of God," Peacock muttered. His heart threatened to beat out of his chest. "This isn't happening."

"Run!" Fija shouted. "Now!"

"No!" John bellowed. "He hunts by movement! Just stay where you—"

His words had come too late. The female warriors were running, leaving the crew of the *Methuselah* far behind. They ran fast, so fast that the men were caught between amazement at witnessing just how cheetah-like they were in their speed and fear because of the deadly predator stalking closer by the second. Snapping out of it, John and Vlad took off running, doing their damnedest to catch up.

"Come!" Fija shouted, finally realizing that Peacock wasn't following on her heels. "Do as I say!"

The Tyrannosaurus Rex stared down at Lieutenant Williams as if it knew he was there. Opening its gargantuan-sized mouth and revealing razor-sharp teeth, it emitted a deafening roar that all but blew his eardrums clean out.

Shaking off the horrid frozen state of shock that had engulfed him, Peacock raised his Laser-5. Unwilling to chance that scientists from his day had been correct and that the king of all dinosaurs hunted solely on movement, he prepared to fire.

Before he could detonate the weapon, he felt two female hands seize him from behind.

"Hold on to my waist," Fija said against his ear. "I've got you."

Lunging down on her thighs, the Amazon shot up into the air in a high-jump that left Vlad and John gawking. The T-Rex roared again, an ear-piercing sound of anger and promised retribution. Peacock on her back, Fija scaled the trees like a monkey on speed, easily outdistancing the horrible hunter.

A blink of an eye later and both Vlad and John were on the backs of two other female warriors, all of thcm repeating the life-saving actions of their leader. A few minutes later, the three men and six women were nestled high in the trees, a hollowed out cavity big enough to shield them all.

"I have never seen any shit like that in my life!" This from a panting Peacock.

"Nor have I," Fija admitted, her eyes round. "I have battled the *loma* and the—"

"I meant you." Peacock's eyes trailed over her face, down to her metallic cup-clad breasts, and back. "You were fucking amazing."

He grinned at her blush, then looked away. His smile faded as he regarded Vlad. The big Russian briefly closed his eyes and glanced away.

"You have my sincere apology," Vlad mumbled. "I thought that surely the gauge had to be malfunctioning."

"What is the reading?" Peacock bit out.

John sighed, adrenaline crashing and fatigue winning out. "Just get it over with and lay it on us. What is the damn reading?"

"100,000,007," Vlad said softly. He looked up, his gaze flicking back and forth between Peacock and John. "B.C."

* * * * *

Their eyes wide with fright, Malik's warriors took a step back as they watched the king-god destroy everything in his path. Bellowing and roaring as though he'd gone insane, he knocked over chairs and sent tables flying as he stalked from the ziggurat.

The human queen had escaped.

"Great One," Ghazi murmured, "I will go with you to find her. Fear not for we *shall* recapture her."

But it was as if the king-god had heard nothing that his most trusted ally had said. The remaining warriors backed up further, giving King Malik Ahmose a wide path as he exhausted his rage. Shifting into his beast form, he flew up into the sky...and off to find the escaped queen.

* * * * *

Leaving Malik had been the hardest thing Alex had ever been forced to do. She realized it was for the best, for she knew she could never, under any circumstances, endure the misogyny of Tongor for a lifetime. And, she recognized with a heavy heart, there was nowhere in Takuru that Malik could be happy.

Romeo and Juliet. The analogy had been more apropos than she'd realized.

Her hand flew to the bite mark on her neck, covering it. Alex wasn't certain what had happened when he bit her, but somehow she felt even more bound to him than what she already had. In a way she hoped the mark never healed. Like a souvenir, it could serve as an eternal reminder of those days and nights she'd spent in Malik's bed.

She didn't regret the time she had spent with him, but conceded that she could never go back. Not so long as the Xandi were intent on enslaving women and robbing them of their minds. So now here she was, trying against all odds to find her way back to the Takuri—a people whose ways she didn't respect any more than the Xandi.

At least in Zala, Alex knew that changes would be coming. They believed she was their queen. So be it. If that was the card fate had dealt her then she would play it to its advantage. The female warriors didn't know it yet, but their morals and life-ways were about to evolve...a lot.

Her breathing heavy, Alex finished winding her way up to the top of a cliff and peered over it. There was a river below, then more land on the other side. She stilled, not too sure but almost positive she saw people on the far bank. Squinting, she honed in on the scene as best she could.

"Al!" a male voice echoed from over the distance.

It was Peacock. Holy shit! It was Peacock. And John and Vlad and...Fija! There were a few other women warriors, too, people she didn't recognize.

Alex's heart began to race. A smile enveloped her face. "Peacock!"

"Al!" She saw him cup his hands around his mouth. "You okay?"

"Yeah!" she yelled back. "But I don't see a way off this cliff."

Fija walked a bit closer towards the river. Even from this distance Alex could see her entire body still—and tense. "You needs must jump into the water!" she bellowed. "Do it! And quickly!"

Alex's forehead wrinkled.

"Jump!" Fija implored her again. "For the love of the gods...jump now!"

A foreign sound, one akin to both gurgling and clicking, reached Alex's ears. The tiny hairs at the nape of her neck stood on end.

Something was behind her.

Afraid to look, but realizing she had no choice, Alex slowly cocked her head and glanced over her shoulder. Oh. My. God.

"This isn't possible," she whispered, her green eyes wide. She was being hunted — pack hunted. And what was hunting her was too incredulous to believe.

"Jump!" she heard Fija scream. "We ran into these creatures two days hence. They cannot swim!"

Raptors. She was being hunted by *Velociraptors*.

Holy son of —

The rest happened as if in slow motion. Alex saw one of the creatures prepare to lunge off its mighty thighs. Whipping around and praying she hit water rather than a jutting rock, she threw herself off the side of the cliff and dove for whatever lay below.

Seconds later, she hit water. So did her hunter.

"Come on, Al!"

"Swim faster!"

"*Mooooooove!*" She heard Vlad bellow.

Swimming against the current, Alex tried with every bit of strength she could muster to get away from the creature and its wildly snapping jaws. The proficient killer might not be able to swim, but it was determined to take her down with it. It flailed closer and closer and…

Her heart racing, adrenaline kicking in, Alex turned in the water to face her nemesis. On a hiss, deadly pikes shot out from where her fingertips were. Fangs exploded from her gums. Not sure what was happening to her, but realizing Malik's bite had made her what she now was, she went with the instinctual pattern that took over.

On a deafening roar, she attacked the creature in the water. The *Methuselah*'s crew and the female warriors stood on the bank of the river. Their jaws were all but unhinged, unable to believe what it was they were seeing—

Alex had turned into a creature deadlier than any they had ever encountered.

Circling her prey, she established her dominance. They struggled for a suspended moment, but then, as if the creature knew and understood its place in the chain of life and death, it offered little resistance when she killed it with a single, lethal slice to the jugular. Blood gushed out from around the dying carcass, staining the pristine silver waters a haunting crimson.

Alex turned her head to look at her crew, her heart beating like crazy when they stared at her as though they'd never seen her before. Taking the cue, she glanced down at her reflection in the mirror-silver waters not stained by raptor blood. She paled.

Malik had made her…one of his kind. She didn't fully shift like a true Xandi, but neither did she recognize the face staring back at her. Her eyes were gold slits, her teeth serrated fangs. She looked as frightening and formidable as any predator.

"Oh my God!" Alex cried, reaching out a hand for help. "What is happening to me?"

By the time her crew reached her in the river, the anger had dissolved and with it her alter-ego. The deadly pikes disappeared as though they'd never been and the fangs retreated back into her gum line. On a blink, her eyes returned to their natural state, light green and round in lieu of gold slits.

"It's okay, Al," Peacock murmured, grabbing onto her. "Let's get to the shore. You'll be just fine."

"What's going on?" she demanded, her voice semi-hysterical. "Were those...*things*...what I think they were? And what about me? What did I just turn into? What the fuck is going on!"

Vlad sighed. "Yes, they were raptors. We have much to tell you."

Alex barely heard him. The shock of what she had turned into during the fight in the river had all but frozen her powers of rational thought. She'd never felt more primitive or base in her entire life. The need to kill had been maniacal, an instinctual thing that couldn't be tamed or described.

When Malik had said they would always live within the other, he had meant it in more ways than one.

Chapter Twenty-One

"100,000,007 *B.C.*?" Alex could only gawk at her men. "Are you serious?"

"Afraid so," Peacock sighed.

"You saw the Velociraptors yourself, Alex," Vlad reasonably pointed out. "And that's not all we have encountered while looking for you."

"The T-Rex," John listed, "two packs of Velociraptors, two Coelophysis—"

"—and a partridge in a pear tree," Peacock muttered.

"That's the Cretaceous Period...I think." Alex frowned. "But people—or our monkey ancestors—didn't spring up until at least five million B.C."

"Well apparently scientists were wrong." Vlad raised his hands. "I do not know! All I do know is this—there are dinosaurs here and there are humans here. The Takuri might be the forebears to humans, creatures that are destined to become extinct, but humans they are."

"Maybe the Xandi and the Takuri are fated to kill each other off. Maybe their fossils are so deeply buried within the earth that scientists from our day never found them." John shrugged. "I don't have any answers. Science is art, a working hypothesis. Nothing is set in stone. You know that, Alex."

Silence.

"It makes sense," Alex whispered.

"What do you mean?"

"The Xandi might not live on in fossil finds, but they live on in human folklore." She went on to explain about how they shape-shifted, describing their two forms. "They easily could have been the basis from which humans derived tales about gargoyles and vampires."

Her crew continued on with the conversation amongst themselves. Being scientists, they sounded like kids who'd discovered Santa's hiding place. All Alex could do as the Takuri-crafted boat whisked through the black waters was feel the heaviness of the burden that had been placed upon her.

If John's hypothesis was correct, the Xandi and the Takuri would kill each other off. The thought of Malik's people dying out was as troubling to her as the thought of Fija's people meeting with the same fate. Once upon a time, she had fooled herself into believing that she couldn't have cared less. But now? So damn much had happened. Too damn much.

She didn't know what she could do to help or if she even should. By entwining herself even further into the fabric of the twenty thousand years-long war that had raged on between the Xandi and the Takuri, Alex could very well be revamping history.

Two races. Two cultures. Both believed themselves superior to the enemy.

How can I fight against that? As Malik said, am I to believe everything can change after a fuck or two?

Sighing, Alex gazed out onto the dark waters as if it held answers. To her chagrin, all it possessed was what it was—a black abyss where the unknown dwelled.

* * * * *

"We know her position, Great One. Let us strike now and reclaim the mortal human queen."

Malik stared down from the cliff out onto the black waters where the small vessel drifted closer and closer to the Takuri stronghold. "She is no mortal. I saw to that."

Ghazi stilled. "You...*what*?"

"I gave her immortality," he retorted without apology. Turning to face his most trusted ally, Malik shook his head. "I cannot do this, my friend. I cannot force her to come back to Tongor against her will."

Ghazi searched his eyes. "If I may be blunt?"

"You may."

"What possesses you?"

Malik smiled as he looked away, back toward the boat that carried Alexandria further and further away from him. "Romeo and Juliet," he murmured, confusing Ghazi impossibly more. "Were it possible to refuse my father and deny my name, I would. For her, I would."

Chapter Twenty-Two

"My queen," Fija said softly, "will you dine with us this eve?" She cleared her throat. "We will permit your males to dine with us, too, does it please you."

"Have you released your son from bondage?"

"I have." Fija's back went ramrod straight. "With gratitude to you for forcing me to do thusly."

Alex blinked. She'd been back in Zala for a month and every day without Malik felt longer than the last. Inside she felt dead, but she forced a smile to her lips so that Fija would know she was well pleased. "I'm happy for you. And for him."

Silence.

"Little warrior," Fija said softly, "all will be well."

Alex's hand absently played with the gold collar she wore. She supposed she should have asked Fija to help her find a way to remove it, but wasn't quite ready to let go. "I'm with child," she whispered. "Malik's child."

Fija stilled. "Good gods," she muttered.

Alex's nostrils flared. For the first time in a month, she felt emotion. It was anger, but she supposed it was a start. "And is that so bad?" she snapped. "Why must the two races be enemies? Why can there not be peace!"

Fija was quiet for a moment, and then, "I heard what you and your males discussed on the boat back to Zala."

Alex's eyebrows inched together.

"It might be our destiny to kill each other off. This is what was said."

"I'm sorry you heard that."

"I am not." Fija sighed. "The women of Tukuru believe in you, my queen. Where you lead, they will follow. Do you want peace between the races, I believe our people will take heed and do your bidding. But it takes more than one race to call an end to the war. I do not see your Malik standing here wanting the same."

Alex closed her eyes against the words. "You are correct," she whispered. Slowly, she opened her eyes and regarded Fija. "What about my baby?"

"You are a strong woman, Alexandria the Great." Fija inclined her head. "You will raise him to be as wise as his mother. Of this I hold no doubt."

Tears that didn't fall gathered in the corners of Alex's eyes. "Thank you." She smiled, this time the gesture not forced. "You are wiser than I will ever be. I owe you much."

"You owe me nothing." Fija walked towards the doors, leaving Alex alone with her thoughts. "I will tell the others you are tired this eve. Get some rest."

* * * * *

Malik had tried to stay away. For a month he had waged war within himself, doing all that he could to give Alexandria the gift she most desired — freedom. In the end he had decided to keep the vow to himself, but not until he saw her one final time.

He had to know with all certainty that this was what she wanted. He had to look into her eyes and see the truth within them. He had to say to her the words of love she had given to him. If nothing else, she would know before night's end what lay in his heart of hearts.

Managing to get past Zala's heavily flanked perimeters had proven a bit difficult, but not impossible. Before Alexandria, his mind would have been racing with the significance of that fact. After Alexandria, it only made him irritated that there was any barrier at all between the two of them.

Tracking her from there would have been easy even if the bite he had given her hadn't made it so he could hone in on her location at any time, from anywhere. She lived in the temple that had long ago been erected by the Takuri; the temple where their prophesized queen was to live and rule.

He found her in her bedchamber, alone and looking unwell. The circles under her eyes were foreign to him so he didn't know what they signified. All he knew was that his Alexandria was ill.

You cannot die, little one. I made you an immortal.

In his animal form, his keen ears picked up a small beating sound as he landed on the balcony of her bedchamber. Curious, and uncertain what it was he was hearing, Malik stilled. The sound came from...

Her womb.

"By the gods," he murmured. "You carry my child."

His heart began to race, a myriad of emotions engulfing him all at once. Elation. Possessiveness. Territorialism. Hunger to be joined with her again.

Fear that she would seek to keep him from his child upon its birth.

Malik stood there on the balcony, shifting into his man-form without even thinking about it. All he could do was stare at her and bask in the beauty that he felt inside. Before her, there had been nothing. After her, he noticed all the things he hadn't before — tears, joy, pain, happiness — *life*.

Alexandria the Great had awakened him in more ways than one.

Finally, after what were long minutes of simply watching her, Malik prepared to make his presence known. Wearing the customary black, thigh-high leather skirt and black knee-high boots of the Xandi kingship, he entered her bedchamber.

Alexandria stilled upon taking notice of him, perhaps unable to believe what it was she was seeing. Or, more to the point, who it was she was seeing.

"Malik," she breathed out, her eyes wide. "What are you doing here?"

His muscles tensed as he wondered if his presence here was unwanted. "I came to tell you—"

Before he could get his entire rehearsed speech out, Alexandria threw herself into his arms and hugged him tightly. He closed his eyes and allowed himself to bask in the moment, to hold this very special woman in his arms again.

"I love you, Alexandria," Malik murmured against her ear. "I couldn't let you just walk away from me without knowing what it is I feel for you."

"I love you too," she whispered. "I've missed you so much."

They hugged for what felt like forever, but not nearly long enough to satisfy. Swiping a rogue tear from her cheek, she backed up and looked him in the eyes.

"Do you still feel the way you once did?" Alexandria asked.

"What do you mean?"

"That you and I are not strong enough to end this war together and bring peace between the races?"

Malik stilled. His gaze searched her face. "You make me believe we can do anything...together."

Her smile was the most beautiful sight in the world. He returned it with one of his own.

"That means," she said, "no more hypnotizing—or whatever it is you do—to Takuri females."

His smile faded. He could well imagine how happy the Xandi warriors would be to hear this announcement.

"On the same token," she conceded, "the males of Takuru are no longer held as slaves."

He didn't smile, but his eyes showed respect for the changes she had accomplished in a mere month's time. "I accept your terms."

"That's only the beginning."

Malik snorted, the first time in his life he'd ever come close to laughing. "I daresay I do not doubt you."

Alexandria gazed up at him. "But we can save that for another time and place. Right now I only have one request of you."

Malik lifted an eyebrow.

"I want my king-god to fuck me."

His cock grew erect at her words. She had a way with him like that.

"That's good," he rasped, "because I'm going to go insane if I don't get inside my queen-goddess' pussy right now."

One minute they were standing there staring at each other and the next they were all over each other, tearing at what little clothing the other wore. "Be careful," Malik chastised as he lowered her naked body to the bed, "do not hurt our baby."

"The baby is fine." Alexandria's eyes widened. "Wait...how did you —?"

"Your king-god knows all," he growled.

She grinned as he came down on top of her, then groaned as he thrust his huge cock in her flesh all the way to the hilt. He made slow love to her, just as he had the last time they'd been together. Just as he would on many more nights to come.

"I love you, Alexandria," he whispered against her ear before sucking it. His thrusts were possessive, branding. "I will always love you."

"I'll always love you, too, Malik." Her smile was voluminous. "Always."

They spent the entire night and well into the next day and evening making love, talking, and planning out the changes that would be forthcoming for Takuri and Xandi alike. It would be a long, hard road, but one they would venture down together.

Alex had been in shock when Malik had informed her of what the bite to her neck signified. Not only could she shift when a predator threatened, but she was now an immortal. She couldn't be killed.

It would take a while for the impact of all that entailed to sink in.

Usually Fija knocked before letting herself into Alex's bedchamber. Tonight, Peacock at her side, she didn't.

"Dinner is prepared, my queen..." Fija's voice trailed off and her eyes widened as she took notice of the uninvited guest lying naked and stretched out on Alex's bed.

Peacock sighed. "Oh boy," he muttered. "Guess who's coming to dinner."

Alex threw her head back and laughed.

Epilogue
One week later

Alex blew out a breath as Fija nodded toward the relic that had been stored for thousands of years inside the Hall of Herstory. Looking first to Malik and then to her crew, she approached the holographic display.

The crew of the *Methuselah* was here for this moment, as were Fija, Malik, and both races most trusted warriors. The uncertainty of what was about to be revealed to Alex and all those present had her insides shaking.

"Go on, my love," Malik murmured. "We needs must know."

She inclined her head. Placing her hand on the scanner, her DNA was a perfect fit for the person that the advanced computer console had been searching for. Within moments, the machine was whirling and a holographic display of the Zutairan man appeared before them.

Alex stilled. He was older than he'd been the last time she saw him — very old and very sick.

"Greetings to you from one year to the day of Armageddon, Dr. Frazier. I have spent my entire adult life building upon what other scientists have learned and, I believe, created the ability to time travel from a singular wormhole in deep space. If years of scientific questing has aided me and what I have done has worked, then you and the crew of the Methusclah entered that wormhole and have reached Earth's distant past rather than its nonexistent future."

Her teeth sank into her lower lip.

"To answer the question foremost in your mind, neither side won the war." His sigh was reflective. "But then, is there really any other outcome to be expected?"

Malik looked down to Alex and then back to the display.

"Since the dawn of recorded history, humanity has waged war on itself in the name of power and greed. In this, the final chapter of the book called New France, both sides lay dead. We defeated the enemy, but we have killed ourselves off in the process. Those few of us that remain are aging at an astronomical rate. Within weeks, all will have perished."

Alex closed her eyes briefly, pained by his words. Malik threaded his fingers through hers and squeezed. She took strength in his presence, just as he took strength in hers. Her eyes flicked back open.

"You have the power within you, Alexandria the Great, to carve out a new destiny for humankind. There can be peace or there can be war, but there can never be both. Each side must learn to give, each culture must realize it is superior in no one's eyes but its own."

Tears threatened to spill as Alex watched the Zutairan man age another twenty years right before her eyes. His voice grew gravellier, his eyes tired and ready to sleep…forever.

"I have lived long enough to do what it is I feel the gods put me here to do. I have given humanity another chance in you. A chance to know love instead of hate. A chance to realize peace instead of death. A chance to thrive instead of perish.

Lead your people with a wizened hand, Dr. Frazier. This way lays death. It is up to you to carve out a new destiny for the world formerly known as Earth."

The Zutairan managed one, final, weak smile.

"Peace and love," he murmured. "Peace and love."

About the author

Critically acclaimed and highly prolific, Jaid Black is the best-selling author of numerous erotic romance and erotic thriller tales. Her first title, *The Empress' New Clothes*, was recognized as a readers' favorite in women's erotica by *Romantic Times* magazine and consistently appears on best-selling lists years after its initial publication.

A full-time novelist, Jaid calls herself "a spinner of fantasies – not a documenter of realities". Known for being an "edge" writer, her work often delves into the darkest realms of female sexual fantasies and brings them to light. She currently writes for Ellora's Cave, Pocketbooks (Simon & Schuster), and Berkley/Jove (Penguin Group).

Jaid lives in a cozy little village in the northeastern United States with her two children. In her spare time, she enjoys traveling, shopping, and furthering her collection of African and Egyptian art. She welcomes mail from readers. You can visit her on the web at www.jaidblack.com or write to her at P.O. Box 362, Munroe Falls, OH 44262.

Other Ellora's Cave Titles by Jaid Black (paperback and e-book)

<u>Multiple Author Anthologies</u>
- "Devilish Dot" in *Manaconda* (Trek series)
- "Dementia" in *Taken* (Trek series)
- "Death Row: The Mastering" in *Enchained* (Death Row serial)
- "Besieged" in *The Hunted* [coming soon in paperback]
- "God of Fire" in *Warrior*
- "Sins of the Father" in *Ties That Bind*

<u>Trek Mi Q'an Series—Single titles</u>
- The Empress' New Clothes
- No Mercy
- Enslaved
- "No Escape" & "No Fear" in *Conquest*
- Seized

<u>Single titles</u>
- "Death Row: The Fugitive", "Death Row: The Hunter", & "Death Row: The Avenger" in *Death Row: The Trilogy*
- The Possession

Novellas

- Warlord
- The Obsession [coming soon in paperback]
- Vanished [coming soon in paperback]
- Tremors [coming soon in paperback]
- Naughty Nancy (Trek series) [available soon]
- Politically Incorrect – Tale 1: Stalked

Why an electronic book?

We live in the Information Age — an exciting time in the history of human civilization in which technology rules supreme and continues to progress in leaps and bounds every minute of every hour of every day. For a multitude of reasons, more and more avid literary fans are opting to purchase e-books instead of paperbacks. The question to those not yet initiated to the world of electronic reading is simply: *why?*

1. *Price.* An electronic title at Ellora's Cave Publishing runs anywhere from 40-75% less than the cover price of the <u>exact same title</u> in paperback format. Why? Cold mathematics. It is less expensive to publish an e-book than it is to publish a paperback, so the savings are passed along to the consumer.

2. *Space.* Running out of room to house your paperback books? That is one worry you will never have with electronic novels. For a low one-time cost, you can purchase a handheld computer designed specifically for e-reading purposes. Many e-readers are larger than the average handheld, giving you plenty of screen room. Better yet, hundreds of titles can be stored within your new library — a single microchip. (Please note that Ellora's Cave does not endorse any specific brands. You can check our website at www.ellorascave.com for customer recommendations we make available to new consumers.)

3. *Mobility.* Because your new library now consists of only a microchip, your entire cache of books can be taken with you wherever you go.

4. *Personal preferences are accounted for.* Are the words you are currently reading too small? Too large? Too...**ANNOYING**? Paperback books cannot be modified according to personal preferences, but e-books can.

5. *Innovation.* The way you read a book is not the only advancement the Information Age has gifted the literary community with. There is also the factor of what you can read. Ellora's Cave Publishing will be introducing a new line of interactive titles that are available in e-book format only.

6. *Instant gratification.* Is it the middle of the night and all the bookstores are closed? Are you tired of waiting days—sometimes weeks—for online and offline bookstores to ship the novels you bought? Ellora's Cave Publishing sells instantaneous downloads 24 hours a day, 7 days a week, 365 days a year. Our e-book delivery system is 100% automated, meaning your order is filled as soon as you pay for it.

Those are a few of the top reasons why electronic novels are displacing paperbacks for many an avid reader. As always, Ellora's Cave Publishing welcomes your questions and comments. We invite you to email us at service@ellorascave.com or write to us directly at: 1337 Commerce Drive, Suite 13, Stow OH 44224.

Printed in the United States
25111LVS00004B/58-225